The Writer's

Block

Joe McClain Jr.

This is a work of fiction. Names, characters, places and incidents are either the product of the authors imagination or are used fictitiously. Any resemblance to actual events or locales or persons, living or dead is entirely coincidental.

ACKNOWLEDGMENTS

The Lord above for this tremendous blessing. The whole Uprock Publication family, DJ Redlite, Kevin Askew, Bri Blue, Ceroromo Bragg, The whole We Major Ent., Ise Lyfe, Paul Mabon, Black Ice, Rodzilla The Blackademic, every Def Jam poet who I have graced a stage with, my parents, my beautiful Queen Chaz, The Dunaway Family, The whole McClain family, The whole city of San Diego, The whole city of East Chicago(IN), the whole 219, 773, 205 and 313. Peace and Blessings.

CHAPTER 1

The time came for me to finally leave my momma's house after eighteen years. In one instance, I was the happiest brotha on Earth. In another, I was more scared than a man whose woman told him that she missed her period. See I wasn't your average teenager. Hell, I didn't really even want to go to college or join the military, seeing that both are systems they try to embed in us from birth as if we desperately need them for survival.

My father had passed away at the age of 12 from stomach cancer. Luckily for me, he was a very prosperous business owner who invested his money well. He set up funds for his loved ones in case of his death. In the middle of my senior year in high school, my mother called me into her bedroom.

"TJ," she said in her usual calm voice. "I need you to see

something."

I walked in the room to see her holding a folder in her hand. I slowly took it out of her hand and opened it up. It was my dad's will. As my eyes scanned the paper, they immediately stopped as I read a statement that would forever change my life.

"To my son, Terelle "T.J." Washington, I leave you $500,000." Nothing else mattered in that will to me but the words $500,000. My mouth dropped as I turned to my mom with an astonishing look.

"Well TJ, what are you going to do?" The obvious answer was to go to college, but I wasn't the average kid, nor did I think like the average teenager like I said before. After about 10 seconds of mind wandering, I gave her my honest feelings.

"Mom, I wanna take this money, go to California and achieve my dream of becoming a published author." I slowly waited for the "you must be crazy" or "lil negro please" words to come out of her mouth. Really, I was waiting for her to slap the dog shit out of me. Ironically, she didn't. She looked at me, smiled and said

"Son, I believe in you."

I didn't know how to register those words, but they slowly sunk in. As my mom continued to smile, I had a quick flashback of why she would accept this. As I began to speak, she cut me off with a valid explanation.

"Son, you never gave me any problems after your father died. You continued to respect me as your mother, you kept your grades up in school, avoided the perils of the streets and you have earned my trust with the decision you made. NOW GO

FOR IT!!"

Was this a black momma talking to me, or was this just a dream? These were my questions sinking in my head as the tears began to flow from my eyes. We then embraced in a hug that seemed like it lasted forever.

***

That June of 2002, I walked across the stage of East Chicago Central High School, graduating and obtaining my high school DIPLOMA. I emphasize the words "obtaining my diploma" because many of my friends just walked across stage and received a blank piece of paper. As I sat and observed the last of my peers crossing the stage, I thought to myself, how many of them would be here in four to five years?

This was a valid question, seeing that East Chicago had a murder rate through the roof. Drugs and gangs plagued this blue collared, steel clad city. I knew that not all of us would make it to see 21.

"Ladies and Gentlemen" our principal Darnell Clark bellowed. "I present to you, the 2002 class of E-C-C!!!!"

We all triumphantly threw our caps in the air. Me in particular, I threw mine towards the door to avoid the ruckus that was too come. As my cap soared though the air, it seemed to hang a little longer and drift. I have always been one to think outside of the box. Was this God's way of telling me that I was about to embark on a slow, yet perilous journey? I mean, why was I thinking this deep? It's only just a cap. It's only just a cap. That's what I kept telling myself, but my spirit was telling me another thing. I honestly didn't know. All I knew was that 12 years of homework, nagging teachers, detention and tardy bells were over. I was ready to embark on my new journey of becoming one of the world's best renowned writers. This life was over, and it was on to the next phase of manhood.

***

My mom got in contact with some of my relatives in San Diego while I enjoyed a few weeks in the summer with my friends. A lot of them were going to downstate universities, so I just tried to enjoy the time I had left with as many of my people as I could.

One in particular was named Ashley Carter. I had met her in my sophomore year of high school. She was a small town country girl from Nebraska, who moved to the city when her mother took a job here. We became great friends. Eventually, we grew into best friends. I was head over heels for this girl. From our turnabout date my junior year, to just hanging out in general, we had fun. Towards the end of July, when everyone was starting to wind down too make sure they had everything they needed for college, she gave me a call. I thought nothing major of it. We talked almost every night.

"Terelle, I need you to come over. We have to talk."

I sensed no urgency or fear in her voice, so I didn't think too much of it. I drove over to her house in the Sunnyside section of the city. There she was, sitting on the steps. My God, she was so chocolate and pretty. Every time I seen her, the feeling of a fat kid eating an over sized cake was there. I definitely wanted to have her as a girlfriend, but I could never muster up the courage during my high school years to ask her.

"What's up skinny doo wop?" I chuckled.

"Nothing much pot liquor!!!" she responded (She gave me that name for sipping juice from a pot of collard greens one night). We talked about everything that calm summer night. Life in the country, the city, where we seen ourselves in ten years. You name it, we talked about it. We sat on that porch well into the night conversing, and then I had an internal rush that resulted in something that I will never forget.

"Ashley??"

"Yessssss," she said in a joking way.

"I-I-I'm in love with you. I've been in love with you from the very first time I laid eyes on you. Over the years, our interactions have done nothing but allow my feelings to grow for you." *Wait, did I really just spew this Romeo and Juliet ass crap off my lips??? Did this really come out of my mouth??? Ahh damn* I thought. This girl is never going to want to talk to me again. She paused. I paused. I didn't know what was going to happen next. Would she leave?? Would she stay?? What??

As tears formed in her eyes, she put her head down. I could see my words deeply affected her. You would've thought I wrote a nasty poem about her and read it to a group of my peers in front of her. It was one of those you hurt my soul cries.

"Terelle," she whimpered out as she looked at me, eyes more red than tomatoes.

"Yes, I love you too." Before I could get another word out of my mouth, she reached over and gave me the most passionate kiss ever. I know we were teenagers, but wow!!! If tongue wresting could create babies, she would have been impregnated with seven of them. I had never ever in my life experienced such a triumphant moment. This is what Kurt Gibson must've felt like after hitting the game winning home run in the World Series. Once it stopped, we both just stared at each other. It was a look as if we could pierce each other's skin and see our organs. She smiled. I smiled. We both hugged one another. Nothing else happened that night, but the intimacy we shared on that level was better than any intimacy penetration could ever produce.

***

August 15th came around. It was the day that most of my peers were heading out and leaving to their new home for the next four years. As for me, I was prepping to leave this city for good and head out West to achieve this California dream. My mom had booked me a ticket for Saturday the 17th, the day after my eighteenth birthday. She and a cousin of mine, a retired Master Sergeant in the Marine Corps, had made living arrangements for me out there. His home would be my home. So many emotions were running through my head that night as I lay in my bed. What was this new life going to be like? Will I succeed?? Will I fail??? Will I get a chick pregnant??? So many emotions crept through my cranium until I finally crashed out.

***

August 17th was finally here, and I was more nervous than a live pig at a Black family reunion. My mom pulled up to the Southwest Terminal at Midway. As I pulled my bags out of the car, I could hear her cries, as she wasn't ready to see her baby boy go. I hugged her with a deep embrace, yet not long enough for her to get ticketed. I swear, these Chicago TSA folks swear they're the FBI. With one last look, she told me some words that etched in my head forever.

"Make your father proud T.J." Not her, but my father.

"I will mom. I promise." She gave me a kiss and off I went. I checked in, got my ticket, made it through security and down to my gate.

"Southwest Flight 3802 is now boarding all passengers." This was it. It was time to become a man. Luckily, I was group A, so I boarded first. As I walked on the plane, I headed to the back and obtained a window seat. I looked at Chicago like never before. I stared at it with a sense of completion. Here I am, an eighteen year old, staring at everything he ever knew. Illinois, Indiana was all that I thought about. Besides those two states, I didn't know what existed outside of it. It was crazy. Here we go I thought. Within 20 minutes, we were all boarded and I was in the air. Cali, here I come.

CHAPTER 2

"Ladies and Gentlemen we are descending into San Diego. Please keep your seat belts on until we have come to a complete stop on the runway. We hope that you have enjoyed your flight, and thank you for choosing Southwest Airlines. We hope to see you again shortly."

Those were my welcoming words into this brand new environment. From the air, I was in total awe. The cloudless sky was just amazing. San Diego's Downtown, unlike Chicago's, looked extraordinary, yet not confusing. And what in the heck was this bridge that I was looking at? All these images were my welcome into San Diego. *From the looks of things,* I thought to myself that *this should be one roller coaster of an experience.* Little did I know that those exact words would sum up everything that would take place after this plane landed for years to come.

***

We finally touched down. I exited the flight and headed to baggage claim.

"T.J.!!!!," a loud and beckoning voiced called out.

"There's my baby cousin's baby boy!!!" It was my retired Marine cousin Barnett. My goodness, did this guy remember that he was not in the service anymore? I mean, from head to toe, he was sharp. He had creases in his jeans, shined wing tipped shoes, a neatly trimmed beard and he talked in a voice that was equivalent to God when he talked to Noah.

"Welcome to San Diego cousin," as he shook my hand with a boa constrictor death grip. We conversed back and forth as we waited for my bags. From how things were going, it seemed like cuz was going to be cool to live with. I also figured that I could learn a lot from him, seeing that he was nearly 40 years my senior.

We got my bags and we rolled out into the city. He gave me a quick tour of the downtown area, which came nowhere near the size of Chicago's. That to me was a great thing. From there, we headed back towards the I-15 freeway, and I witnessed the shock of my life. SIX LANE HIGHWAYS!!! I looked at cuz and screamed it.

"Cuz, you guys have six lane highways!!!???"

"Aint that what you see!!!???," he bellowed out. I couldn't believe it. These folks had six lane highways out here. Wow!!! San Diego had great weather, all the room in the world to drive and a beautiful downtown. All I could think of was what's next?

We exited the freeway, and caught the light.

"You hungry cousin??"

"Indeed" I responded. Cuz then drove to a Mexican restaurant about a half mile down from the exit ramp. I had never been fond of Mexican food, seeing that at the crib, the only thing we cared about was deep dish pizza, pizza puffs and White Castle's. Walking in, I could sense the pride Mexicans took out here with their food. I mean, Cali was once Mexico, so that wasn't a shock. I scanned the menu, not knowing what to get. Screw it.

"Can I have the surf-n-turf burrito please?"

I didn't know what the heck a surf-n-turf burrito was, but it sounded like something out of Hawaii. I was handed this huge, gigantic log of a burrito wrapped in aluminum foil. All this for $6.00 I thought. Cool beans. We walked back to the car, jumped on the road and I took my first bite.

"GOOD LAWD!!!," I shouted. My cousin laughed hysterically.

"That's some good eating aint it cousin???"

"Hell yeah cuz!!!," I responded back emphatically. Boy, this was some good stuff. I damn near had an orgasm with my first bite of this.

We pulled up to Barnett's house and I was immediately awestruck. This was a huge house, nestled in the confines of great scenery and peacefulness.

"Wow cousin, this is amazing."

"Thank You," he responded.

"This area is what they called Mira Mesa. It's quiet, peaceful, the people are friendly and you don't have to worry bout no mumbo jumbo, trunk rattling bullshit that some of you youngsters do."

I knew the military would come back out of him with some cursing sooner or later. As I walked into the house, I noticed many awards, plaques and a framed Marine uniform. I didn't know what any of those stripes meant, but it was a lot of them, so I assumed he did a damn good job while in there. Once I got my bags settled in my new home, cuz and I sat down in the living room for a long talk. We chatted on my goals, his accomplishments, my upbringing in East Chicago and life back when he was young.

This went on for about two hours. Finally, near the end of our conversation, cuz said something I will never forget.

"T.J., listen up. I respect what you are doing in trying to achieve your dream. However, I need you to remember three things. One, the same pitfalls that plagued Chicago, plagues here. This is not all of San Diego. Just like Chicago has a ghetto. We have a ghetto. Two, be careful of the company you keep. ESPECIALLY THESE WOMEN!!! These California women are not like Midwestern women. They live totally different. This isn't the country bumpkins you're used too. These are the fast life girls, who live at a fast pace. They'll ride and suck ya dick until they get 18 years of child support money shooting out of it. This is how Southern California is. Third and most of all, remember this if you don't remember anything else. You and only you are responsible for your outcome. Not me, not my neighbor, not the bum who tries to wash your windshield at the stoplight, not the first piece of ass you get out here. You and only you are responsible. I am not saying that you will fail, but know that all roads that lead to success are bumpy. It only gets smooth once the goal is achieved. And after the goal is achieved, there will be a new obstacle, with even more bumps in that road."

Wow was all that I could think. Hearing these words from a man who served 28 years defending this nation had me looking in a different direction. Not only was I now re-energized to accomplish what I came out here to do, I was now looking at an even bigger picture. First, I would win over California. Then, I would win over the entire United States. Last, I would have the world at my fingertips. YES!!! I felt like Scarface in my head. This is what all those years of late night writing were adding up too. As the night progressed, Barnett's words echoed in my head. I was focused. I was ready. Tonight, was my rebirth. As I finished the night off with television and some good ole grape juice, all I could think about were the things to come. This was my time and my time was now.

***

The first few weeks of my arrival were spent adjusting to and learning my way around the city. Cuz had three cars that were paid for, and he allowed me to use one to get around. I kept things simple at first. I drove around the Mira Mesa area, locating the simple necessities such as the grocery store, restaurants and entertainment venues.

As I got adjusted to that area, I branched out and began to really discover San Diego. Pacific beach looked like the spot where everyone partied. I hit Mission beach, and I found women of all shapes and colors. Mission and Fashion Valley were a jewel of their own. I was amazed so far. However, my touring mainly consisted of up and down the 8 and 15 freeways. I was ready to expand. Going into my fourth week in the city, I hit the 5 freeway and started to head south.

I discovered the suburb of Chula Vista. This was the other San Diego that cuz must have been talking about. It wasn't run down or anything like that. However, the vibe did change. It reminded me a lot like East Chicago. I started to see more mom and pop stores down here. Plus, it looked like a mini version of Mexico. I kept it simple and cruised down Broadway, until I headed back West towards the 5 freeway. I rolled back up north, catching the California breeze. Man I thought, this life is going to be great. I had no complaints so far. Everything was going as planned.

Next week, I would start going out to venues to try and get my name out there with my penmanship. I was going to simply take the 15 back home, but something told me to continue going further. I drove until I seen an exit for the 94 freeway. Martin Luther King Freeway was the name to be exact. Hmmm??? Back home I thought, MLK Street is the one place that no one wants to be. However, San Diego was so beautiful to this point, that I thought the city had just named a freeway after a great man. I took it. I rolled up the freeway, noticing nothing out of the usual. I seen an exit sign to Euclid Ave. *What the hell,* I thought. I'll take it. I got off and slowly but surely, I saw what my cousin was talking about. I was definitely in the hood now. I saw the quality of homes diminish. There were more barred windows than a little bit. Hoodrats with skittles for hair doos and dusty niggas with saggin pants and nappy cornrows were walking around like it was nothing. I thought to myself, *remember to turn back around on this street and get back to the freeway.* I kept going until I hit a four way stop. I observed the street signs: Euclid and Imperial. Oh yeah, I was definitely in the hood. This intersection looked like four corners of death for some reason. It was like you could damn near smell the stench of death. I calmly waited at the light.

As I waited, a group of gentlemen came out of a liquor store to the left of me and began to cross. They were some typical hood niggas. Saggin jeans, over sized tees and Jordans. This particular group though had green bandanas hanging from their back pockets. They passed my car and stopped. They all looked at me, and one shouted out:

"SUP BLOOD!!! YOU KNOW WHERE THE FUCK YOU AT???!!!"

Damn!!! I had gotten myself into some deep shit.

CHAPTER 3

I sped off through the light and damn near took a few cars with me. I kept hearing those dudes scream, and then I felt something hit the car. I didn't care though. I just wanted to get out of there with my life. The whole time I was speeding, all I kept praying to God was

"Jesus, let me find a highway. Jesus, please let me find a highway."

Eventually I did find the 805. I didn't know if it was gonna take me to the 15, but I didn't care at the moment. I was concerned about getting the heck up out of dodge. I didn't stop for anything until I was back in front of my cousin's house.

I walked around the side of the car to see if any damage had been obtained. I noticed a mark with some missing paint. *Ahh damn* is what I thought. Cuz is going to kill me. He was probably gonna ring my neck like the pansy ass recruits he used to tell me about. I stared at the minimal, yet significant damage for a minute, trying to think why these guys would randomly single me out. I looked, I thought. I looked, I thought. Then it hit me. Those guys were dressed in damn near all red from head to toe. This car is royal blue. These guys had too have mistaken me for a Crip more than likely. I couldn't believe this. Back home, we had colors, but we didn't take it to this level. It was a whole different ball game back there. Now, I see I was in a place where a simple color could mean the difference between life and death.

"What's going on youngster?," my cousin said as he walked out of the house, slippers and all. I explained to him what had happened. In my head, I was prepping myself for the biggest ass chewing, and possible ass whooping of all time. Ironically, that didn't happen.

"Are you okay?," he asked.

"Yea, I'm fine." He could tell I was still visibly shaken.

"Remember I told you that San Diego had another side too it? Well, you met it."

Boy did I ever. Cuz kept me calm and took me inside the house. In there, we talked about the gang culture of California and the mentality of the brothers in San Diego in general. He had a lot of insight, seeing that he began a career working in the federal prison after he had retired out of the Marine Corps. After about an hour long conversation, he headed out, while I sat and pondered my next move. Wow, what a hell of a first month out here in sunny San Diego. Two months had now passed and I pretty much had learned a good portion of the city. I knew where to go, where not to go, which color to wear when I'm in a certain area, the whole nine yards. It was time to spread my craft around this city. Online, I had found numerous spoken word venues and coffee shops that hosted open mics where I could advertise and hand out free copies of some of my old writings. They weren't professionally published as in nationwide, but with the help of some teachers from my high school, I managed to get two of my stories professionally put together. My mindset was that eventually, I would catch a break and my words would land in the hands of a well known publisher.

North Park, an area in SD which had a lot of venues was my primary target. I began by stopping in the local coffee shops and just conversing with customers to see where their interest in writing and art lie at. A lot of people blew me off, but there were some who actually took the time to listen. Heck, I even started to enjoy different brands of coffee. I had never been a fan of coffee, but once I sipped a Mocha Latte, I was hooked. I continued this for three weeks. I stopped in at a few open mics just to hit stage and let people know who I was.

Handing out free books and my business cards, I kept telling myself that my big break was coming. I waited for the phone to ring, but it never did. This continued on for weeks and weeks, until those weeks turned into months. Luckily, the money that had been left by my dad allowed me to live well while trying to catch my big break. Time continued to pass and eventually, 2003 was upon us. I had no crazy incidents, cuz was still good and I was still out and about, slanging my books in hopes that someone would give interest. On one late night in January, my phone rang. This would be the call that would change my life forever.

***

"Is this Terelle??," a shallow, yet business like voice deemed.

"Yes sir, this is he. May I ask who is calling??" "This is Dean Johnson, and I own a publishing company out here in San Diego."

I couldn't believe it. After months of going from venue to venue, my hard work finally paid off. Thank you Jesus was all I could think in my head. Mr. Johnson and I talked for about an hour. We chatted about our upbringings, favorite authors, favorite foods and all the good stuff that people who just met each other talk about. We set up a meeting to discuss the parameters of things and see if we would do business together. This is what 6 years of passion amounted to.

I didn't write until my father passed, but I didn't find it as my true love until my junior year of high school. All I could think about was the story that my English teacher Mr. David told me years ago. Burglars once broke into his house while his entire family was there. They were threatened with their lives, but by the grace of God, they only ended up taking material possessions.

As he explained that story, I noticed he did it in an upbeat way. I asked him why this was so. He explained to me that even in the midst of hard times, something great can come out of those times. In his case, his bond with his wife and children grew even stronger. In my case now, my love for writing grew stronger because I now knew that with hard work and dedication, anything is possible.

***

Mr. Johnson and I met a few days later at a very upscale restaurant. His presentation was great. By the end of the meal, I was locked in to having my first book published. The cost for publishing, printing, touring with book signings would all be covered by the company. That was more than good news for me. I had never published anything professionally, so I thought I would have to come out of pocket with some outrageous cost. We went back to Mr. Johnson's downtown office and signed the proper papers. He wrote a small advancement check, and everything was on its way to becoming great.

The story he bought off on was called "Word War III," which told the story of a young black man's struggle from the inner city to the mountain top of success. He said reading it opened him up to a world that he knew existed, but not necessarily understand. I quickly took a trip to some stores that sold some nice dress clothes. I ended up spending $4,000 in all by the end of my spree.

Sport coats, slacks, three piece, two piece, crocs, ostrich, gators, lizards, snakes, fedoras. You name it, I purchased it. I may have been eighteen, but I had enough sense to know that when you're about business, you have to have the look of a business man. No one would take me serious as an author if I were to show up with a white tee, baggy jeans and some Jordan's that had been re-released for about the 7 billionth time. Those days were still there for me, but not right now. I would save that look for my out and about days. For the next few weeks though, I concentrated on strictly business.

***

It took about two months, but my book was finally ready for consumers. Mr. Johnson was great and held up to his end of the bargain. I was well promoted in national magazines, newspapers and media outlets alike. He set me up with some interviews up and down Southern California that would air on each city's local media outlets. It was fun. I was getting the word out there about my book, and I felt everything was falling into place. However, my biggest surprise came returning to San Diego from Long Beach. I had my face on a billboard. A BILLBOARD!!!!

Who would've ever thought in a million years that a black man from East Chicago's Harborside face would be on a billboard, and it wasn't someone wanted for murder. I couldn't believe it. I had finally arrived to the big time.

My first signing was at a Borders bookstore in San Diego. Honestly, even with all the advertisement, I expected a semi-descent crowd. Man oh man, was I wrong. The line was wrapped around the corner. Mr. Johnson looked at me with a wide grin and said

"It's your time. Enjoy it."

Enjoy it was what I indeed was going to do. I greeted, signed and conversed. I tried to keep everything short and brief, seeing that I had a lot of people wanting to get signatures. Occasionally though, you would get caught up in a 2-3 minute conversation. I had everyone from every race there. Every kind of person you can imagine was there. Fat, skinny, dark, tall, short, even a few midgets got their books signed. Four o'clock rolled around and it was time to wrap up. Just as Borders were about to shut it down, I heard a voice yell out

"WAIT!!" It was a young black woman, walking fast to approach the table.

"Do you have time for one more??," she asked.

"Yes I do," as I tried not to stare at this sculpture of beauty God carved out of pure chocolate himself.

"Who am I making this out to beautiful?," I said in the smoothest voice ever.

"Karey sweetie." My God, not only did she look sexy, she talked sexy. She was clad in a beautiful red dress. Two diamond studded hoop earrings graced her ears. Her smile could awaken King Tut out of his gold casket. The only thing that would be better is if she came in ass naked. We chopped it up for a good while at the table, and our vibe was great. Eventually, we decided to exchange numbers and continue this talk some other time. Man oh man. First book signing, major success and I met one of the sexiest women Southern California had to offer. In Cube's words: "TODAY WAS A GOOD DAY!!!"

CHAPTER 4

The first results of my book sales had come out after a few weeks. I had the #1 bestseller in the country. Damn New York. I was #1 in the country!!! I could have kissed a duck in its mouth at that point and yelled **AFLAC!!!** My first check came in after that, and wowzers!!!

I had seen a lot of zero's due to the money that my dad had left me. These however, all belonged to me. I was grateful. I immediately got on my knees and thanked God for his awesomeness. I immediately thought what I was going to do with my first check which read $140,000. Off top, I knew I would place $14,000 into an organization committed to doing God's work of helping the less fortunate. Next, $26,000 was going into a new account I was opening up. I would never touch it, allowing it to just sit and collect interest. Next, it was time to head out on my own and get my own place. I now knew that I would have a regular source of income, so it was time to give cuz his space back. Everything was going great. However, not even my first check or the thought of moving out on my own kept me happy. All I could think about was Karey. Her, that red dress, that priceless smile, that lil tattoo I seen that creeped out from under her dress. We had stayed in contact on pretty much an everyday basis since we met.

She was 19, a Leo like me and was in school at San Diego State as a sophomore majoring in communications. She originally hailed from Tuscaloosa, Alabama. You could tell she was indeed a southern belle. She stood about 5'5, with dark chocolate skin. Her body was proportioned correctly, and she was thicker than a pot of grits with butter and salt. For you slow folks out there, she had an ass to die for is what I am saying.

She was the sweetest and most mature woman you could meet. I wondered how she could be nineteen, but carry herself as a much older woman. I called her to tell her the news of my book. She was more ecstatic than me. Just the way she supported me in my endeavors made me feel at peace. She was definitely the icing on the cake. It had been about a month and a half after my book signing, and we had grown closer everyday. During our conversation, I asked her out on another date, but I didn't tell her where I was taking her.

I arrived at her campus apartment in my newly purchased Mercedes Benz. It was smooth driving, pretty and black like she was.

"Oh wow," she said as she walked out the door down to meet me in some fitted jeans and a blue top. My goodness that ass was phat.

"When did you get this?, she exalted"

"I got it two days after receiving my check and I thought it would be a great idea for me to take you out in it." She smiled, grabbed my face and gave me a great kiss on the lips. We weren't official, but it sure as hell felt like it. By the end of the night, I knew we would be official though.

I took her to a nice, serene joint on the coast near downtown called Island Prime. We both felt the energy as we enjoyed great seafood and each other's company. As the night progressed, I told her my feelings. I asked her can we become official, because I didn't want to let her get away.

"You are my man. No questions asked," as she leaned over the table to engage in a nice peck. This was great. I was now an established author, in a great city and had started a relationship with a beautiful woman. In a little time span of almost a year, I was on a great track. We decided to walk along the waterfront after dinner. Hand and hand, we talked about everything.

She told me about how it was to grow up in country ass Alabama. I told her about the perils in my city. We talked about where we saw our own individual selves in ten years. Most of all, we were really interested in learning each other on all levels. After a stop and gaze session at the moon, where we also shared a lot of deep, passionate kisses, we headed back to the car. We drove around downtown and Coronado, sharing laughs and singing random songs that came on in the car.

This was one night that I wish would never end, but I knew it had too. You couldn't have asked for a more perfect night. The stars were out and I had the biggest one of them all shining in my passenger seat. Eventually, we ended up back at her apartment near campus. I walked her to the door, said a few words and we kissed. As we kissed, she pulled me inside and slammed the door behind her.

The more we kissed, the more clothes got ripped off. It had been a long time since I had been with a woman, being so focused on business and all. That shit was over, and I was about to get it in.

"I'm bout to show you how Southern women treat men who handle their biz," she whispered. As she said that, she pushed me down on her bed. My shirt was already off. My pants were unbuckled. She was down to her bra. She was tattered up, but didn't overdue it. She had one that crept up her entire right leg and OMG that shit was sexy. Her shoes were somewhere and I didn't care where. She pulled my pants down aggressively, pulled my dick out and with one huge wad, she spit and started slurping. I couldn't believe this.

Man, I had received some head before, but she inhaled my meat as if it were some ribs at the Taste of Chicago. She sucked ferociously, yet tenderly. Licking and sucking my balls and all. She stopped to stand up, smile at me and take the rest of her clothes off. Thank goodness she did too. I felt like I was gonna pop off from that vacuum cleaner mouth. I followed suit and laid back on the bed.

"NO!" she yelled. "I'm on my knees. Stand over me and push

your dick to the back of my throat!!!"

All I could think was *what the hell???* I had never had a female like this, but I was going to respect her wishes. I slid my fingers through her hair and pushed my dick all the way in. She moaned, with a little cough, but she wasn't affected much. I had found me one who for the most part didn't have a gag reflex.

YES!!!! She enjoyed this domination, as she occasionally pulled my dick out her mouth, laughed and said do it harder. She continued to suck me furiously, tears drippin down her face, every now and then yelling out for me to fuck her face. After a while, I couldn't take it anymore. I pulled her mouth off my dick, grabbed her sloppy face, kissed her, picked her up, threw her on the bed and buried my face into that pussy.

With the first lick, my head started spinning. Her pussy tasted like water. No scent, no odor, just pure, 100% USDA certified good pussy. She talked dirty to me and grabbed my ears as I licked her down thoroughly. Her moans and "Oh fucks" were confirmation that I was licking this monkey right. I felt her legs began to buckle. Her breathing got heavier. The "OH FUCKS!!" started to get louder. All this happened until she eventually let a gush out all over my face and halfway down my throat.

THIS CHICK IS A SQUIRTER!!! I never in my life had one of those.

"COME HERE AND FUCK ME!!!," she yelled. I slowly came up and slid inside of her real slow. It was the equivalent of a human entering a sauna. Her pussy was tight, juicy and warm. We fucked aggressively, challenging each other. This was the type of stuff that I loved. I thought Chicago women were some freaks. These Southern girls had them beat by a clean mile. Sweat poured from our bodies as we tried to out do each other. She talked shit. I talked shit. She loved when I pulled her hair as I killed it from the back. This was the heavyweight bout of the bedroom.

As she rode me on top, bouncing that phat ass up and down, she said in a soft yet demanding voice

"I wanna taste you." Before I could even comprehend what she had said, she jumped off and started sucking me as if she were trying to get the cure for cancer out of my dick. I tried to maintain, but not even thirty seconds after she started, I was releasing. She kept sucking though. I couldn't see it as my eyes were closed.

I was convulsing, and my body was tightening up. I raised my head slowly to see her licking up the drops that exited her mouth and landed on my skin. She then went back to sucking on the head. I moaned out a breathless moan, as I was sensitive as all hell. She looked at me, gave me a devilish laugh and continued to suck until I went completely limp. She then ran her tongue up from my stomach to every inch of my chest. She climbed up, looked me in my face and whispered

"to the shower."

We sped to the bathroom. It was more of a freak session than a shower. After the soap suds wore off, we engaged in some deep passionate kisses and body touching. Eventually, I got back hard and she dropped down to deep throat me as the water ran down both of our skin. Eventually, we went at it a second time. From the bathroom, to her living room couch, we did this. We gave each other what we wanted, until I pulled out and came all over her face. I wasn't even thinking. I thought she was gonna kill me. However, the way she was rubbing it in her skin while playing with her pussy, I could tell she enjoyed it. We shared a laugh as I wiped her clean, and we proceeded back to the bedroom. The sheets got changed, the fan got cut on, and we lay under the covers and just held each other.

I know it was too early to say anything involving the word love, but this is what it felt like. Damn, how did I luck up like this? Get a good woman who is 100% lady in the streets, yet unrecognizable in the bedroom. I guess it was just my lucky day. My eyes slowly started to drift, and I crashed out like a newborn baby. Things were really on the up and up now, and I had received the greatest nut from a woman from the dirty dirty. Life was good.

CHAPTER 5

A year had now passed. I authored an additional novel, and it sold very well. The money was rolling in, and everything I had dreamed of in life was taking hold. I had purchased my own condo, toured several venues across the states and I also surprised my babe with a new car. The 2004 Mercedes e500 to be exact.

She would graduate this year after only three years, and I was hoping for her to move in. Until then, she kept the same apartment on campus just to avoid the daily strain of driving back and forth to school. Our relationship had blossomed. We fell deep in love with each other. What kept us going was the fact that we never stopped falling for each other. It was like a first date every time we were together. We'd cook for each other. She massaged my back. I massaged her feet. We did random stuff like go to Toys-R-Us, buy some super soakers and just shoot each other outside in a random park. It was amazing. Not to mention the sex. Our lovemaking and all out fuck sessions were a twenty on a ten scale. There was never a dull moment, as we explored new ways to keep each other satisfied on the physical tip.

Spiritually, we both believed in God and knew it's against his will to have sex before marriage. It's hard though when you love each other like we loved each other. I was slowly preparing to propose to her after she graduated. I wanted everything lined up perfectly with us. Also, it wouldn't make any sense now, seeing that I still had some tour dates and signings to attend. 2004 was here with a bang, and I foresaw bigger and better things for both of us. Nothing was stopping me. If something did try to stop me, I was going to run through it with a vengeance.

***

My tour of the Southern part of the United States had started. I never went to the South as a child, but it had always intrigued me. Reading the stories of the slave way of life in school perplexed me. I thought, how could any race of people force another race of people to live in such horrible conditions? Furthermore, how could any human being look at himself in the mirror, knowing that he is physically, mentally and emotionally destroying another human all in the name of a profit? It saddened me to think about such travesty. My tour started in Jackson, Mississippi at Jackson State University. Aside from normal book signings and appearances, I wanted to ensure that I talked to peers around the same age as I. Not every nineteen and twenty year old you see is on the verge of becoming a multi-millionaire, all while living their dream. More importantly, not every nineteen and twenty year old has the power to impact and influence others to strive for a positive way of life.

Black males my age were looked upon as thugs or gangsters for the most part. I hated that notion, but it was the way of the world. I wanted to show these young brothers that anything was possible, as long as you kept God first and applied yourself to what you wanted to achieve. The stereotype could be beat. This was a great opportunity for myself.

I bounced around to every Southern state and touched every major city in the South. From bookstores, HBCU's, normal colleges and business seminars, I was there. Hell, if I could talk at the hood liquor store I would. The best part of all this is that I was impacting lives on a huge scale. I kept in contact with Karey on a daily basis, making sure she was good to go with her school and anything that she may have needed.

I talked to her about how blessed I was with this opportunity. She gave me strong moral support and always asked me is there anything that she could do more of to help me. I had a great team of business minded folks around me, but just hearing her ask about my needs in regards to my career made me love her even more. I was almost home to her. This tour was almost done. Plus, I was kind of jet lagged from traveling state to state. I needed to get back to California to sit on my own couch, lay in my own bed and grab my nuts in peace. I had one last stop which would last three days. It was a place that I always heard about. People called it the chocolate city of the South. They said once you go here, you would never want to go back to where you were originally from. That place was Atlanta, Georgia. Or, as us youngsters called it HOT-LANTA!!!

***

This city was amazing, and I hadn't even stepped foot into the city. As I landed at Hartsfield-Jackson Atlanta Int'l Airport, I damn near broke my neck. Hell, I thought I would be cross eyed by the time I left here. The airport was stacked full of beautiful women. Whether they were TSA workers or just travelers passing through, they were some stunners. If Chicago women were Apple Jacks, then these women were Frosted Flakes!!! They were beyond great!!! Oh boy is what I thought to myself. I had to handle my business and get up out of this place. I felt like the devil was sitting on my shoulder saying, "Gotcha!!!" Real shit, I didn't even wanna leave the airport. From my observation, it looked like the party was in here. Good God Almighty!!!

I had no time to rest. After checking into the airport hotel and eating a quick meal, I was busy scanning the schedule. I had a 7 p.m. over at Morehouse. It was twelve noon luckily, so at least I could catch a few winks before I had to get up and do my presentation. I took that nap, threw on a Navy blue suit with baby blue pinstripes, some Navy blue Ostrich skins and headed out to kill this joint. Morehouse was great. Talking to those young black men really appealed to me. During that presentation, I thought about East Chicago.

The only time I seen a group of men all dressed the same back home, were if they were being shown in the County lock up, or they were on the street corners, sagging their pants while destroying their own community by selling drugs. As far as being neat and presentable, that was irrelevant. I thought to myself, what if one day I can be that example? What if I can inspire the young men of my hometown to dress to impress in a business like manner, and not one that would attract flashing lights? It was merely a thought, but it was a very powerful one.

The second day had seen more of the same action as the first. This day however was jam packed on my schedule. I was starting fresh at eight in the morning at Spelman University. Follow that with a one o'clock at Clark Atlanta, a six o'clock at Georgia Tech, and I knew I would be making love to the bed tonight. The first presentation went well. I sold books, gave insight to these young adults on how to achieve success and handed out business cards. With two hours between that and my scheduled appearance at Clark Atlanta, I had time to enjoy some official Waffle House. My PR rep Mark was originally from Atlanta, so he ensured that I would get a taste of the dirty dirty as he called it. Finally, I arrived at Georgia Tech. To my surprise, I wasn't presenting myself to a typical auditorium crowd. They were having me present in the main gymnasium of the basketball team.

This was crazy I thought. I would be presenting in a place where some of basketball's best had played. Kenny Anderson, Stephon Marbury, Chris Bosh. Man, this shit was crazy. Speaking with the chancellor of the school, he informed me that many students had read my writings and demanded that I come here to speak. There were so many students who wanted to hear my message that the gym was the only place to fit them.

Wow I thought. Now that's what you call making an impact. All 8,600 seats were filled at the start of my presentation. Out of all the venues I spoke at, this one had to be the best. The crowd and I all spoke to each other through our eyes. I have never seen a group so large, all focused with the intent of hearing a message. There were college crowds, and then there was Georgia Tech.

***

My set there ended at around 7:30, and I winded down the next hour or so signing books and just conversing with students. At some time during my book signing, a young lady came up to have her copy of my second book "Mirror Image" signed.

"Who shall I make this out to Miss lady?"

"Doesn't matter," she replied. I kind of chuckled at her response as I signed her book: To whom it doesn't matter. Terelle "T.J." Washington. As I handed her the book, she candidly took it, gave me a deceptive stare and slipped a card out of here blouse sleeve on the table. She walked away biting her lip. Now, I can't front. Shorty was bad as all get out, but my focus wasn't on women right now. I calmly took the card, placed it in my pocket as I thought nothing of it and continued signing books.

The night ended totally for me around 9:30. After rapping with the chancellor for an additional thirty minutes, I was ready to unwind and just relax. I wanted to head back to the hotel, but Mark had other plans for me.

"Bruh, lets hit Strokers!!!" I couldn't believe this dude wanted to hit the strip club after this long ass day we had. Three schools. Thousands of students. After all that, and this dude still wanted to see some naked ass.

"Mark, bruh, I'm tired. I just wanna get to the telly and rest up."

"NAW MAN!!!," he yelled as if I was down the street. **"LIVE IT UP!!!!"**

"Fuck it," I said hesitantly. "Let's go."

We hit the strip club and hot damn!!! This was the Atlanta I had heard so much about. This was a Nelly tip drill video live and in person. All I needed was my credit card to swipe through a pair of plump ass cheeks and I would've been straight. I was sleepy as hell, but I woke up quick. We stayed in Stroker's well past three in the morning. I didn't drink, but Mark was faded. I don't know what he was seeing through his liquor vision, but I was seeing 100% USDA quality approved meaty cheeks.

Boy, A-T-L women had some serious backside. I wasn't gonna do like all the crazy rappers and blow 100 stacks on some naked bitches. I did however, take out some twenty's and fifties to toss em on stage. It was the closest I would ever feel to being a rapper in my life. Before we left, I headed to the bathroom. Crazy how a trip to the bathroom seemed like a trip through the jungle of pure nakedness.

As I was about to wash my hands, I reached in my pocket and found the card given to me earlier. *I WANNA FUCK* was written on it clear as day. I laughed at that shit as I just tossed that thang without a care in the world. I washed my hands, got Mark and we headed back to the Marriott.

It was well past four now, and almost five. I had a bomb time at the strip club, plus I was full of some Jack in the Box. With supreme croissants to be exact. I was sleepy as all to be damned. Luckily my last speaking event wasn't until seven in the evening that day, so I could get plenty of rest and be refreshed for my last go round. As I began to lie n bed, I heard a knock at the door. *Who in the hell could this be?*

"Who is it!!!???," I screamed. No answer. ***BOOM, BOOM, BOOM***. Three loud knocks was all I got. All I could think was this better be the old man from Publishers Clearing House saying that I won $1 million dollars a year for life. I went to the door, slung it open and it was ol girl from Tech. She was in a trench coat and blue heels.

"Remember?"

Ahhhh damn. Here we go with this shit.

CHAPTER 6

"Yeah, I remember you. The fuck you doing at my room at this hour?" I said this as if I didn't know. This chick really was on one. A million thoughts were running through my head. The biggest one of them all though was how did this chick know where I was staying at?.

I heard of stalker chicks, but this one took the cake. I didn't know how this was going to play out, but I had to devise something fast.

"You know what I'm here for," as she nudged me into the room, closing the door behind her and dropping her coat to reveal a matching royal blue thong and lace bra set. Now, I can't front, she was thicker than a pot of gumbo with extra shrimp. I seen her at Tech, but that wasn't nothing compared to what I was seeing now. On a normal day, I would've beat the breaks off this pussy. This wasn't normal though. I had a great relationship and everything was going well for me professional wise. I did not wanna fuck anything up.

"Lay down," she said. "Let me entertain you and run this." I had only a matter of time on how I was going to handle this. My girl quickly ran through my head. I never even considered cheating on her, but boy was this tempting. It's not everyday that a Lion can get a free meal without having to hunt. Hell, even Simba wasn't stupid enough to pass up Nayla when she came back into his life in The Lion King.

Also, considering the fact this was an ATL product, I could pretty much guarantee she could fuck like a champ. I laid down and executed my strategy in my head.

"Hold on baby," in my Barry White voice. "Let me run this shit."

She licked her lips with acceptance and whispered "Yes daddy."

I grabbed her ass and threw her on the bed. Damn, that soft ass skin of hers didn't make it any better. I put on a strip show for her. I could see she was getting aroused as I dropped every article of clothing on me, until my basketball shorts and this one measly little chest tattoo was all that showed. I climbed on top of her, letting her caress me. I blew soft breaths on her skin. Damn, I needed to be careful. I was trying to play it cool as a part of my plan, but I was getting to the point of where I wanted to knock the dust off of this pussy.

"You want me mama?"

"Yes daddy." I asked her again.

"You want me mama?"

"Yes daddy!!!," as she said it a little louder.

"I got something for you girl." I got up to get a black bandana I slept in at night.

"You ever been blindfolded?" She shook her head no, even though I knew this freaky ass girl was lying. I told her to rise up and sit on the edge of the bed, yet don't touch me. Having her face so close to my hard dick was exciting her. I could tell by the way she was nibbling on it through my shorts, trying to absorb the pre cum that was already drippin out my shit.

Aaah shit!!! Lord, please don't let me slip up was what I was saying in my head. I slowly put the blindfold around her eyes, picked her up from the bed, spun her around and grabbed her from the back. With a slight grip around the back of her neck, I walked her to the wall near the front door, where I threw her against it just hard enough to get her aroused, but not enough to hurt her.

I grinded my dick against her while whispering sweet nothings in her ear. To get her going even more, I whispered a quick erotic poetry piece to her:

"As your vines slowly wrap around my trunk seeds get implanted to spawn new growth unless that growth is deep rooted in the throat and your tongue lathers up the juice of life"

Now, I had dabbled with poetry in my day, but it wasn't no shit I took serious. However, it damn sure came in handy then. She couldn't take it any more, as she started begging me to fuck her.

"You ready baby??"

"YES!!!,"she shouted. **"FUCK ME NOW!!"** I had this bitch on cloud nine. Just then, I grabbed that still unlocked door, picked her up and launched her ass into the hallway.

"STAY THE FUCK OUT MY ROOM BITCH!!!" I quickly grabbed her coat and slung that mutha fucka too. **"AND TAKE THIS SHIT WITH YOU!!"** *BAAM!!!* I slammed, and locked the door then called hotel security to let them know that it was a crazy, naked bitch out in one of their hallways that needed to be escorted out. I even called the police to file a report, just in case this heffer was crazy enough to say I Mike Tyson'd her.

Even with doing that, my nigga side kicked in and was yelling "DAMN!!!" It's hard to turn some cooch down. Especially some down south cooch. Shid, Karey was from Bama, and her shit was like a tight ass flowing waterfall. You know the pussy is good if it sounds like eggs getting beat in a bowl.

If hers was like that, I can only imagine what these other women's in the South was like. By the time the police came, she was long gone. I told them the whole story. Luckily, it was two brothers. They laughed as they explained how this always happens in the ATL. They always get some calls about crazy ass hoes trying to jump on the long dick express of all the famous cats that roll through here. By the time all this was over with, it was well past six in the morning, and my black tail was going to sleep. I had one last event later in the day, and enough excitement for one night. Dreamland was calling.

***

I woke up around one in the afternoon still a little groggy, but I couldn't sleep anymore. I had one more stop at seven, and that was for my last presentation at Georgia State University. I packed all my bags, as I would be flying out immediately when the event was over. Around 2:30, the limo picked me and my PR up, and I told him about the events of last night.

"Man I would've smashed."

I shouldn't have expected anything else from Mark. He was a businessman, but he was a hound at the same time. If pussy was served at a McDonald's drive thru, he would be there every hour on the hour getting the McPussy value meal with extra cooch sauce. All I could do was laugh as we made a quick stop at Sonic for some chicken sandwiches and chocolate shakes. From there, it was on to GSU and then back to Cali.

***

After killing GSU, everything wrapped up around nine o'clock, including signings and all. My private flight back was scheduled for 11:30. All I could think about was sleep, sleep and more sleep. More importantly though, I thought about Karey and how she was doing. I debated about whether or not I was going to tell her about what happened. I never hid anything from her. At the same time though, this was something serious that could derail our relationship. Then, I thought about what one of my uncles who was in The United States Navy told me.

What happens overseas, stays overseas. I know this wasn't overseas, but he was right. Everything that happened in Atlanta was going to stay in Atlanta. I loved my baby, but I wasn't about to risk getting my dick cut off. We got to the airport, checked our luggage and eventually boarded. Aaah, there was nothing like a private jet. All the privacy and drinks I wanted. After this wild Southern tour, I would truly need me a few of them. Not to mention that this flight was five hours and some change. After take-off, I smashed a good meal, drank four Henn and Cokes, and my black tail crashed all the way until we hit San Diego.

***

I touched down in San Diego around 4:40 in the morning. My girl was there to pick me up, but she could obviously see that I was dead tired and just wanted to go to sleep, even though I had slept a good three hours on the plane. We got my bags, rolled to the car and headed to the taco shop by the house. She knew I needed to have my surf-n-turf burrito fix after three weeks away. I swear those thangs had drugs in them. We discussed everything about my trip on the way there, including that crazy woman who tried to get me. I didn't even mean to tell her. The convo was just flowing so smoothly that it just came out.

She chuckled as I explained detail by detail the events of that night. That response brought relief to my soul. It also taught me the importance of honesty in a relationship. Even the stuff that you may be scared to tell your partner, you should tell them.

Before, I told myself that everything in Atlanta would stay in Atlanta. However, she had a right to know. We pulled up to Cotixan. I got my surf-n-turf burrito and headed to my condo in the Scripps Ranch area of San Dog. As we lied down in bed, Karey began to stroke me gently.

"Not right now baby. I'm tired."

"Naw boo," she said. "None of that. I figured that. You were

42

honest with me bout everything, so the least I could do is suck you to sleep and get my medicine at the same time."

Hot damn I loved this woman.

***

Over the next few days, I took time to relax, settle back in and spend time with my lady. My team and I were good for quite some time with all the profit I made off of that book tour. We stayed informed with each other via phone conferences, as our next big venture was to plan the marketing of my next novel. However, for the rest of this month, which had 16 days left in it, we were all just going to live and let loose.

I did a lot over the next 16 days. I went to community centers to assist with writers workshops. I shopped for more suits, ate more Mexican food and went crazy in the gym. Above all that, I spent time with the only other woman out here that I considered like family. Over my course in San Diego, through a mutual friend, I befriended a woman named Jackie. She inadvertently became like a second mother to me.

Helping me out on my journey in SD, we became close, as did the rest of her family and I. Hanging out with them was fun. There was never a dull moment. Her grandson Darrell inadvertently became like a nephew to me. You talk about a simple child? All this kid wanted to do was eat, play video games and stay fresh. Have any of you ever met a young kid under the age of ten that had a bottomless pit for a stomach? Or a kid who had to have creases in his clothes? Or a kid who only wanted to hit up Chuck E. Cheese as a reward for getting A's and B's in school? Yea, me neither. They were truly a blessing to be with.

***

Nearing the end of the month, the hottest party crew in the city was throwing a party. Anytime We Major Entertainment threw something, you could expect three things: women, fun and good music. The first expectancy was the key for me. Hey, I might have been locked down, but that didn't mean that a brother couldn't look. Lucky for myself I wasn't a hound, cause they damn sure kept some stunners at their party, and I know for sure I could knock a lot of em down.

Anyways, I knew those boys for a while, so anything they had, I supported. I clocked out downtown to the Red Circle. It was a small venue, but efficient enough to throw a party. I chopped it up with my mans Blocko as soon as I got there. I was really proud of this brother man. He was one of the first cats I met when I arrived out here. He had really expanded his brand and turned it into something to be taken serious. It was good to see black men doing positive things.

The whole night was crackin. Bottles popped all night. Bird, Fresh and Moe kept it tight on the ones and two's. Everyone was having a blast. Ass was shaking here, there and everywhere. CLAUDE!!! Around 2 a.m. the party ended, and everyone started to file out. More than likely, they were headed to Denny's or Jack in the Box, seeing that those were the after club spots out here. I was out in front of the venue choppin' it up with one of the homies. We noticed a group of men across the street conversing. We thought nothing of it. Hell, you know how everyone does after the club. They just sit around and talk for a good minute before they head off anywhere.

POP!!! POP!!! POP!!! POP!!! POP!!! Gunshots started to ring out!!! Everyone took off like roaches when the lights came on, trying to avoid being a victim. Hell, the whole downtown was dippin out it seemed like. Cars were being brought to immediate stops because of folks running through the streets. I didn't know where the shots were coming from, but I ran and ran all the way until I got to my car. Shid, Forrest Gump would've been jealous of me. By the time I reached my whip on 6th and Market, I could hear the police sirens. *God don't let anyone I know be hurt* was all I could think. It would be a damn shame if a great night ended on a sour note with the unfortunate death of someone.

I skidded out that parking lot at warp speed, being careful not to appear as if something happened to the lot attendant. I didn't want her taking my plates down and callin the cops on me. I turned out the plaza and hit the light. I was gravy. I escaped and was still trying to catch my breath. All of a sudden, I felt a burning sensation in my leg. I looked down and seen blood.

"WHAT THE FUCK!!!" I yelled out in agony. I had been shot. Shit!!!

CHAPTER 7

AHHH!!! I screamed constantly as I raced towards the hospital. Damn, I thought that I left this ratchet ass fuckery in East Chi. Red lights were not important right now, as I feared for my life. People think shots to the leg aren't serious. However, they forget there is such a thing as a carotid artery. If a bullet hit that, you may as well tell someone to get you the finest marble casket ever.

I knew for damn sure I wasn't ready for my momma to see me as a stiff, so it was all or nothing to me. Burning and in pain, I managed to get to Scripps hospital right outside of downtown. I hobbled in screaming for help. To be even more honest, I crawled through the doors, seeing that I couldn't put any weight on my leg. By now, my blue jeans were all red and my right leg went numb. I wouldn't wish this on my worst enemy. The docs scooped me up, put me on a stretcher and rushed me into the ER. Seeing all these lights and masks messed me up mentally. Worse than that, not knowing if I was going to die or not had my brains scrambled. All my clothes were now cut off and I was staring at nothing but doctors. We were conversing with each other, but deep down I was scared as ever. After what seemed like forever, I was gassed up and operated on.

The bullet was removed and I was expected to make a full recovery. It became lodged in my thigh, but luckily it didn't hit anything major. The muscle would be sore for a while but I was alive and expected to make a full recovery. My girl was contacted some time during my operation. I woke up to her teary eyed over my bed, rubbing my head.

"Babe. Babe." She kept saying that as the tears flowed from her eyes. I couldn't blame her. I could have easily lost my life.

"I'm okay beautiful. Truly I am."

I tried to console her with those words, but it was to no avail. All she did was cry more.

"I love you T.J," as more tears drowned her face. I grabbed her and hugged her as tight as I ever could. All I could think about was the first time I met her at that book signing. I never saw us getting to this point. Maybe, just maybe we would become good friends. However, she became my best friend. Now, more than ever, I was determined to give her the world. It is truly amazing how life can play out sometimes. One minute, you're saying hi to someone. The next, you are making passionate love to em. The next, they are looking at you in one of your most vulnerable states. Wow, Thank God for a great woman and some bomb ass medical insurance.

***

I recovered at home over the next few weeks after my release. Crazy as this may sound, it actually turned out to be a good thing I got shot. I got to just chill out and enjoy the comforts of home. This wasn't just time off where I would use time to go party and volunteer. Naw, this was me just being able to be a home body and actually do for me. Besides the times that Karey was there cooking for me and giving me comfort, I actually improvised and did a lot around the crib.

Hell, a brother even tended to the garden out back. Yea, I didn't grow a damn thing, but to a brother from the hood, weeds actually looked like something. I trimmed em up and made the soil around em look nice and neat. Crazy I know, but it made me feel good. I thought everything would continue to be normal, but to my surprise they had gotten worse.

I randomly had the news on a few days after the incident. As a brother was cooking up some links with some grits, I heard some stuff on the news that drew my attention to the fullest. According to reports, the shooting downtown was gang related. One man was killed, and a few more injured. That wasn't the worse though. When the newspaper ran the story, they had me as one of the people wounded. However, an anonymous source claimed that I was the intended target, saying that I was part of the Skyline Bloods, and rivals wanted to kill their quote on quote head in charge. What the hell? I was a gang leader? An author? Really? I was a brother from East Chicago. Born and raised. I had never seen a Blood or Crip until I got out to California. Hell, back in East Chi, we used to think those were rap groups when I was coming up.

We thought Snoop Dogg's rap group was called the Crips. We had a whole 'nother culture over in the Motherland. Vice Lord's, P-Stone's, Disciples, Kings, 4CH's all came to rise before a Blood or Crip was ever thought of. Hoover, Barksdale, Fort and Bobby Gore was who Chi cats idolized. Hell, even the OG T-Rodgers hailed from Chicago. He got permission to start the P. Stone Bloods from the Main 21 council. It wasn't a People Nation established when he started them up, so they went under the Blood umbrella. I could not believe this. Overnight, I went from one of the top authors in America, to public enemy number one.

I had to fix this as soon as possible. It wasn't no way in hell I was gonna let someone who wanted attention with a lie to mess up everything I had. I immediately got in touch with my team for a totally different reason. I had to fix this monster image that some people were now looking at me as. True, I never cared about what people thought about me. However, when it affected my money, and the ability of me and my lady to eat, then it's a problem. I now knew what major celebrities went through. I wasn't a Jay Z type figure, but I was still well known and had affected many people's lives. I was eventually set up for an interview on local San Diego news. This was great. Not only did I have the chance to explain this situation, but this was the perfect opportunity to clear my good name once and for all.

I arrived at Channel 10 studios the following week for the

recording. As I was introduced onto the show, I felt locking eyes from the audience that I couldn't even see. I already had to hear the mouth of my mama about this. Lord knows if she could watch this, she could probably stare a hole through me. I had a feeling that some people were skeptical. Immediately, the anchor went into the situation with the first question.

"So, as you already know, everyone wants to know what happened on that fateful night." I explained it thoroughly as possible. From the moment I arrived, to the moment the fat chick in the club fell for suffocating those heels, to when I was running for my life, to the roach I noticed outside on the side of the building. I told it all. At the end of my response, I looked in the camera and yelled:

"I AM NOT GANG AFFILIATED!!! I AINT EVEN FROM SAN DIEGO!!!! I KNOW ABOUT CHICAGO STREET LIFE!!! HELL, I WRITE DAMN SUSPENSE NOVELS!!! GANGSTERS DON'T DO THAT"

That last line I felt was my lifesaver. Plus, it gave the news anchor a good laugh. It was obvious that this is what I needed. By the end of the night, I felt my name was cleared, and I was ready to move on with my life. This was further more solidified by the crazed crowd who waited outside of the studio to get pictures and autographs from a brother. I just hoped that the rest of America would follow in their footsteps.

I now began to move on to bigger and better things, like my relationship and my next novel. I was no longer worried about the club situation, or the person who came up with that bogus claim. They were probably sittin on their couch miserable that their bogus story didn't cause me any harm. I was drawing my focus on my newest project entitled "The Writer's Block." It was going to be a story about a writer who dreamed of making it out of the slums of America to achieve success as a writer, all while beating the odds of the new world he was entering.

I had my game plan laid out as to how I was going to construct this work of art. I called Karey up to see if she could come over and help me think of some good ideas. I always liked other's opinions when it came to my books. You gotta remember that when you selling something, value the opinions of others and take constructive criticism. Those same folks are the ones who will be buying your product, not you.

My baby arrived, and we went over notes and plans about my book. My God, she was great. She was calm now after everything that had went down. After we laid out ideas for the book, I cooked her favorite dinner. My babes enjoyed smothered rabbit, smothered potatoes, and green beans. Throw in some butter pecan ice cream for dessert and she was good. We then watched TV and eventually, we ended up in the Jacuzzi relaxing.

Relaxing didn't last long though, as we began kissing, touching and eventually getting down for the get down right there in that thing. It was nice for more than the fact she was the love of my life. The sky was clear, the stars were out and I was almost fully healed . The temperature was right. What better setting could you imagine for making love to the woman that you would one day make your wife? What am I saying? We weren't making love. We were fucking!!! Sometimes, you gotta do that fellas. Women want that. Yes, they wanna know you love em and appreciate em. Every now and then though, you just gotta pull her hair, caress that ass and knock her kidneys out of place.

***

As the weeks dragged on, progress was being made something serious. The book was coming along great. Karey was nearing her graduation date. My team's marketing strategy was put into place. I couldn't ask for anything more. I called my mom back home to see how everything was going. Ever since I had gotten shot, she insisted that I call her everyday. That's when she wasn't blowing up my phone. She was just being a mom and I understood that. Even though sometimes she would get those chills up her spine and call me at 2 in the morning, I didn't mind. If I had a child who had got shot, I may have been doing the same thing.

Everything was good back there. Nothing much had changed around the city. It was the same BS violence, high unemployment and the same BS corruption going on. Hell that was the whole Chicago-land and Northwest Indiana area. They were pretty much two in the same. Crooked ass politicians, no jobs available and high crime rates. People who were there always talked about how tired they were of the city, but yet they didn't do shit to try and make it better. Crazier, they talked negatively about the people who left, including me.

Talking about folks like me don't come back and think they too good for the hood. It wasn't that. It was just that I seen there was life outside of East Chicago and I enjoyed it. People in the hood always want money, money, money and gimme, gimme,

gimme. The best way to me is to leave and make something out of yourself. How you gone rep your city if you never left your city? If you go somewhere and make it, that's how you truly help your city. You are giving others the impression that there are good folks who come where you from. You're letting them know that every black or brown person coming from your area don't sale drugs or throw up gang signs.

I got off the phone with moms and resumed life as normal. The book was coming along well and everything was gravy. I was at the midway point of the book when I stopped to go and get me a surf-n-turf burrito. Boy, those joints were like food's version of crack. As I was leaving the restaurant, my phone rang. It was Karey.

"Yes my love."

"T.J., we need to talk?" I went to the car to continue this convo, and also so I could smash this fire ass burrito.

"What's up babe," I said rudely as hell with a mouth full of food.

"T.J., I love you dearly and I want to spend the rest of my life with you." This I already knew, but I just wanted her to come out and say what she wanted.

"What you need babe?"

"I don't need anything but to hear you promise me you'll be here forever." I did exactly as she said, as I went in to sink another bite of heaven in a tortilla.

"T.J., I'm pregnant." All of a sudden, all the food fell out of my mouth and into my lap.

"Can you say that one more time babe?" in a suttle voice.

"I'm pregnant."

Outside, I was in shock. Inside, I was happier than a pig in a pile of shit. All I had left to say was one thing to her.

"Karey. Beautiful. You two will never have to want for anything as long as I am breathing." I could sense the excitement she had through the phone. I couldn't believe it. I was going to be a father. We talked for a little while longer, and then I headed home. As I pulled into my driveway, I broke down and cried. All I could do was think about my deceased father. Right then and there, I made a promise to him that I would never leave his grandchild in any way. I was going to do all that I could to ensure his grandchild had a better life than me. More than that though, I was trying to envision what the next nine months would be like.

I had to prep myself for the mood swings this woman was about to have. That's what women do when a life form all of a sudden stretches out their body. It was cool though. I had to be there for her no matter what. Even if that meant getting yelled at sometimes or taking a boot to my skull, I was going to be there. She was the mother of my child, and she would be treated as such. Still sitting in the car, wiping the tears of joy away,

I started to think if I had a boy or a girl. It really didn't matter, seeing that all I wanted was a healthy baby. If it was a boy though, I'd be happy because my name would be carried on. Plus, I only had to worry about one thang. If I had a girl, she would indeed be a daddy's girl. However, I know that I would be at the gun range a lot, seeing that I would probably need a lot of practice for these little bastard boys who would come along and try to get my baby.

Hey, I was once that little boy. I know what crept through little boys minds when it came to girls. I just got out the car and walked in the house. I was thinking about too much at one time. I just needed to concentrate on what was important: Being there for Karey in every way to make sure her and the baby would be okay. This indeed was the best day of my life.

CHAPTER 8

It was now 5 months into Karey's pregnancy, and a doctor's visit summoned all my worst fears. I was having a daughter. I'll be damned. Naw, it wasn't nothing scary, as all I wanted was a healthy baby. However, even though I wasn't a wild kid growing up, I had my fair share of adventures with women. All I could think was that all the nasty stuff that I once tried to do with someone's daughter was going to come back on me ten fold.

Shid, all the nasty, freaky, beyond wild shit me and Karey did. All I could think was that my daughter was going to have some of those same traits as her freaky ass mama. Yea, I would definitely need to go gun shopping in the future. All shotguns, no pistols. If any little boy thought he was going to have a chance with my pumpkin, he had another thing coming. I'd blow his nuts off and use them as ice cubes in my lemonade. Right now though, it wasn't time to think like I was a mafia member. She wasn't even born yet. When she hit 10 though, that's when the little grown girl syndrome kicks in. I could relate too this from the many nieces I had. My sisters on my daddy side had popped out some monsters. Even with that, I only spoke to one coming up, and that was my sister

Rene. The worst out of all of them was my niece Amaya. I never met anyone with such a snotty attitude. This girl always whined and complained. You couldn't even talk to her without an argument ensuing. Hell, the first time I met her she acted like her shit didn't stink. Five minutes after seeing me, she proceeded to jump in my bed and pound the back of my neck. Lil Heffa!

I remember one trip to the mall with her when she was five. My sister was finally home from completing a successful naval tour of Japan. She was in the Navy, and had decided to get out and pursue a new life for herself. This was really cool at the time, because I had only seen her and my niece a few times up to that point. I took Amaya to River Oaks mall out in the South Suburbs of the city.

Now really, you couldn't even call Calumet City a suburb, cause that joint was just as ratchet as the Chi, if not worse at times. Anyways, we scoured the mall for about two hours. She wanted any and everything she seen, but a teenagers money can only go so far. We finally descended upon a Disney store, where she seen a princess castle.

"Uncle Jr.!! Uncle Jr.!!! Uncle Jr.!!!" She pointed and shouted non stop until I picked it up and bought that thing for her. We got home and I told her don't open it until she got home with her mama. Did you think she listened to me?? Hell to the no!! That little heifer broke that box open and commenced to trying to put the castle together.

"Uncle Jr., I need your help?"

"NO MYA!!!," I screamed to the top of my lungs. **"I TOLD YOU DON'T OPEN THAT THING TIL YOU GOT HOME!!!!"** She wasn't hearing that, as she whined and cried about wanting to build the castle with me. We went back and forth like two old people until her mama came and picked her little spoiled tail up. If that's what I had to look forward too, I knew it would be a long eighteen years. Thank you Mya for cursing me you little bad ass adorable girl.

***

Along with the upcoming birth of my daughter, my book "The Writer's Block" had flew off shelves and had been selling out everywhere nationwide. With this success, I started to think about change. I was great at writing novels, but I knew I could accomplish more. They say you will never know what you can do with your life until you get up out of your comfort zone. Writing was indeed my comfort zone, but if I wanted to excel, I knew I had to test new boundaries to see where I fit in. One night on a slow weekend, as I sat at home with pregnant belly snoring like a damn freight train upstairs, I decided to write my very first poem entitled Simply Love:

"I wanna catch every tear drop from your past on

my tongue, just so they wouldn't hit your skin cause then you'll only be adding salt to your already open wounds, I wanna consume the leftover food that your last man left in your heart's refrigerator, just so it wouldn't spoil and clog up your arteries, causing you to block my attempts at loving you, see love is beautiful but still painful at the same time, I know heartbreaks can be like water main breaks, spilling over into the streets and cracking my concrete, even though I left the manhole covers off my sewers to divert the flood of your pain, still, your overflow was too much as I couldn't contain everything your heart left out.

see you were left out, with doubts and with fears, and all I had left to give you were my two ears to listen to what your spirit told me it needed to heal, so my touch became life sized band aids and my actions became Neosporin. I started forming a mold of what this was to become, and scraping the scab of that old bum off of you, cause the old saying is true, good sex don't make a relationship last, cause what's the use of a girl having some good dick if none of her orgasms have emotion behind it...its nothing but a bunch of screams for rescue, and vibrations and shaking from being scared to open up her heart again, see men, real men, they love deep, that type of love where while you sleep we keep our eyes open out of fear that the second we close em, we'll wake up and you'll be gone, real men love a woman deep, so deep that she'll find a way for her period to stop, because she don't want her friend to come visit in town when you're around, cause other females like to take what they can't have, just like a tampon takes over a vagina for a week, see loves makes a woman weak to wandering thoughts, cause love won't cause her mind to play Russian roulette with her heart, and true love from a woman makes us do it all, but those with hard hearts call us pussy but its cool, I am what I eat and she loves it...see love will make you do some crazy things, but the biggest thing it does for two people, is make them one"

I looked at this after I finished and thought wow, this looks pretty good. Then again, I thought to myself, don't nobody wanna hear this lubby dubby shit. I could spit this to my girl, but if I spit tis to a group of bruhs they'd roast my ass. However, I held on to it since I wrote it. Now, all I would have to do is hit a spoken word venue and cut loose. There was only one problem. I never recited poetry a day in my life.

I couldn't tell you how to read it, how to say it, how it was supposed to look. None of that. I realized writing a book and sitting in front of a room giving a motivational speech was very much different than getting on stage and giving a full blown performance, all while shifting my voice tones and making the crowd believe my words. They both may sound similar, but trust me; they are two totally different things. Oh boy, this was going to be a whirlwind of a new world I see. God help me, because I sure as hell was going to need it.

***

I decided to ride to the North Park area of San Diego one night and hit up an open mic to test out my skills. There was only one problem. Which open mic would I go to?? This was coffee shop and arts heaven in San Diego. It was damn near an open mic coffee shop on every corner. Nothing really stood out. Everything looked the same. Coffee shop, full of people, someone on a microphone. Damn, how could something I thought would be so easy turn out to be so difficult? I eventually came upon a venue called Queen Bee's Arts and Culture Center. Just to my luck, they were having an open mic on this lovely Tuesday night. It was called Train of Thought, and that's exactly how my thoughts felt once entering this place. All I seen was a bunch of people I didn't know. It was like walking into a new school you just transferred too. Hell, I was so nerve wrecked that I even gave my $5 cover to the cashier shaky as hell. I sat down somewhere in the back row, hoping that I wouldn't be noticed.

This show was like a runaway train. The show started off smoothly with the host opening up with a soulful tune that combined spoken word with neo soul. This looked something that I would enjoy on a regular. After a few house rules were explained, he got into the portion of how they greeted new comers on stage. He would shout

"This is their first time!!!" The crowd would follow with, "We got you!!!"

Ah hell I thought. That would be my introduction into this madness. I was thinkin about walking out at that point, seeing that I didn't like all that attention on me. Funny aint it. I love the attention when I just talk. To perform though, naw. Unlike a speech, you can get booed off stage for not giving people a great performance. Oh boy, this was goin to be quite a long night I thought. After the first two performances, I decided to go and put my name on the list to perform. From the looks of it, I would be going up probably within an hour.

"Coming to the stage next, we got some new blood. Let's welcome him properly y'all. This is his first time. Give it up...for T.J.!!"

What the hell??!!! I swore it was a million people in front of me. Damn!!! I got up like an old man from the wheelchair. It felt like I was losing my virginity all over again. I rolled on stage nervous as hell. This was a whole different ball game for me. Looking out into all these unknowns was destroying me inside. I was so nervous that I didn't even acknowledge them. I just pulled out that folded up piece of paper, opened it up and started reading.

I was choppy with my words, sweating and I was messing up bad. I was waiting for an apple to be thrown at me, or a big ass cane to yank me off stage. I finally finished. Expecting to hear boos; I was very shocked when the crowd gave me a gracious applause. What the hell were these people smoking I thought???

Did they mistake me for someone else? That really made me feel better as I headed back to my seat to enjoy the rest of the show.

After the show was complete, I was able to talk with the host, who went by the stage name of Suge Knice. It was funny, because he was as big as Suge Knight, and had a beard like him as well. All he needed was a bald head and he would've been complete. He told me that my words were powerful, yet if I wanted to really touch the crowd, he said memorization was the key. Also, I would have to learn how to alter my voice tones to make my words stand out and seem believable to the people. That advice really helped. I thanked him, we exchanged business cards and I headed out to the car. I just sat there in the driver's seat for a minute. I started to think of how relieved I was for this night to finally be over. I was so nervous, but things turned out better than what I expected them too. As I pulled out and drove back to the street, my phone rang. I seen it was Mark, but I was wondering what the hell was he calling me for at this damn near midnight hour.

"You need me to get you from a girl house," I chuckled.

"Bruh, get to the hospital!!!! Karey been rushed to the hospital!!!!"

My heart immediately sunk. I aint know what the hell was going on, but anytime someone's rushed to the hospital in the middle of the night, shit is serious. Immediately I started to think about the night I got shot. I would lose my damn mind had the same faith occurred to her. Karma had a funny way of rearing its ugly head back at someone. You ever seen some stuff happen to someone else, only to have it turn around and happen to you in an even worse way?

That was the feeling I thought. Hell, thats all I could think of that happened. Someone had shot my love, or hurt her real bad. A mother fucker was gone get it, just not now. I had to focus. We stayed on the phone as Mark directed me to Scripps off the 163. I pulled up to the hospital ecstatic. I knew she wasn't having the baby because she was only 5 months and some change. What the hell could've happened to my baby?? I sprinted out of that parking plaza like a chicken sprinting from a group of niggas on Super Bowl Sunday. I made it to the ER lobby, only to see Mark and some of Karey's friends with distraught looks on their faces.

"WHAT HAPPENED TO MY GIRL???!!!," I yelled with tears coming down my face.

"WHAT THE FUCK HAPPENED TO MY GIRL???!!!" Mark immediately drug me outside of the hospital, seeing how two uniformed staff officers were coming because of all the commotion I was causing. I ain't give a shit about those rent-a-cops. Right then and there, I would've whooped they monkey asses too. Outside Mark explained.

"Bruh, we don't know. Karey cousin was with her and said she started bleeding real bad."

Miscarriage is the first thing I thought. Damn, this was something that I didn't want right now. All this preparation for my new baby girl, and now it looked like I had lost her. I tried to just bear the news as he gave it too me, as I sunk in a squatting position.

"Where's Karey bruh?," I whispered out with my hands cupped over my mouth.

"She with the docs man. I'm sure she okay, but I'm sorry bout ya daughter man." He picked me up and gave me a hug. It was good to have your peoples around when you needed them. I had always been a strong minded individual who took negative news well, but this was a beast of a different breed. I lost my daughter. I knew it. I could feel it. Now, I had to concentrate on getting my love right mentally, because you just don't recover quickly from the loss of a child.

As Mark consoled me, we all were still anxiously awaiting the news from the doctor. I wish these fools would hurry up. A little over an hour later of me getting there, a doctor came walking out through the doors. He had some blood on his coat and he looked a bit distraught. I already knew he was going to tell me that I lost my lil girl, so that wasn't nothing. At this point, I wanted to know how Karey was. Wasn't shit I could do about the baby, but my lady, that was a different story.

"Are you Terrelle?"

"Yes sir, I am. What happened?!" Just then, doc put his hands on my shoulder and took a deep breath.

"Karey had a miscarriage."

"I figured that man. How is she doing?" Doc slowly took his hand off my shoulder and looked into my eyes with a new demeanor. I could tell what he was about to say wasn't going to be good at all. "In the process sir, she lost a lot of blood. We did everything we could, but I'm sorry. We lost her."

My heart sank as I collapsed to the floor screaming. Her friends were trying to pick me up as they were drowned in tears as well. I wasn't having it. I couldn't believe this. The love of my life, my Karey, was gone. I literally blacked out amongst all the screaming. Flashbacks started to occur of the first time I met her. The first time we argued. The first time we kissed. The first time we did every damn thing.

I don't know how many tears I cried, but I'm pretty sure if Lake Michigan dried up, I could have filled it back up that night. I don't know how long it was, but I came too with docs, Karey's friends and Mark around me, holding a tissue to my nose. I cried so much that my nose had started to bleed. They helped me up. Still keeled over, the tissue was pulled from my nose as I analyzed the blood. If only this was the amount of blood my baby could've loss.

"Let me see her," I whispered. "Let me see her." A female nurse then said sure. I had to prep because I know damn well this was something I did not start off my day prepared to do. Doc walked us all back and up the elevator. We got to whatever floor, and she stopped us all once we got out of the elevator. The nurse was a sister, so I felt a little more at ease, seeing that she may be able to keep us at bay.

"I'm going to let you know, I can let all of you see her, but not all in the room together."

Teary eyed and all, everyone complied. At the same time, they all agreed to let me be the one inside of the room with her and they would look from a distance through a window. We made it to room #801A.

"Ahhhhhhhhh!!!," one of Karey's cousins screamed as she fell to the floor in agony. I seen her through the glass. Blanket covering up her body with only her head exposed. I never seen

Mark cry, but dammit he was even droppin waterworks now. At this point, I couldn't even cry right now. I had a range of mixed emotions from sadness to anger. We all looked through the glass as the nurse slowly escorted me in. There she was, lookin peaceful and at ease. I gingerly ran my hand across her hair and whispered out God knows how many "I Love You's" to her. This shit was surreal to me. Even the nurse started sniffling as she seen me caressing Karey in her state.

"Was she your girlfriend sir?," nurse asked in a raspy voice from crying herself. I paused for a minute, as her question rang through my cranial. I was so perplexed at looking at Karey's body that I didn't even comprehend the question. Or so I thought.

"Naw, she wasn't my girlfriend. She was my best friend. My wife and I was the dummy who waited too long to give her my last name."

As I broke down and put my head to Karey's chest, I could hear and feel everyone come in and console me. Even the nurse was hear like she was family. I whispered out one last

"I love you Karey," and against my will, I was exited out of the room along with the rest of Karey's family and friends. It was official. At 1:27 a.m., on this dreadful Wednesday morning, the love of my life ascended into a new life. Now, the question would be, what would my life ascend to from this point on?

CHAPTER 9

"How could they talk about hell burning
When hell had to feel better than this
fire would actually be a comfort now
since all I see is salt water
running from my eyes
fire is actually welcomed."

I wrote that and a million other pieces throughout the day. I barely slept. I went to the house alone that morning, and wanted to remain that way. The only time I talked to anyone that day was when I talked to Karey's parents. Out of respect, I was going to let them handle the funeral arrangements. They were going to allow her funeral to proceed out here, and later have her body delivered back to Alabama for burial. They did this to give all of her college friends a chance to say goodbye to her as well. I thought that was very humbling of them. It's already hard enough as a parent to be burying your child. To be concerned about the feelings of theirs during this difficult time showed their true character. I sat in the house over the next few days. No TV, No radio and I barely ate any food. I had a billion missed calls. I did not want to be bothered at this point. The only thing I did was grieve and write. Grieve and write.

Losing your father was one thing. Losing the love of your life was totally different. I felt like God reached his huge God hand into my chest and just ripped my heart out for no reason. They say that everything happens for a reason, but I ain't gone lie, people could keep their God talk to themselves right now. I was angry at God. I didn't wanna hear a damn thing about God. At least not right now. I was trying to bear with this loss. Anything that I was working on, it came to an immediate halt.

This was my time just to sit and drown in my own sorrow. What did she do to deserve this? I really sat in my house and pondered that. A self educated and book educated woman who had the world at her fingertips. Yet I could go on that campus any day of the week and see half naked women who weren't worth a pot to piss in walking around freely and loose as ever. This was total and utter bullshit in my mind.

"FUCK YOU GOD!!!," I yelled out at the top of my lungs. Then, I just collapsed on my living room floor and cried. How could I be mad at God? He brought her in my life. I was just going through it though. I would apologize later. I just needed to vent, because I felt my biggest blessing had been snatched. I had it all. A great career. Money. Love. The big crib in the hills. The good life. All of a sudden, none of that mattered anymore, as all I could think about was the fact that I just lost the most important woman in my life next to my mother. Hell, I lost two women for that matter. My unborn daughter was never to be. I don't know how long I cried for, but my tears could've formed a new Nile River. Now, I had to prepare for the ultimate, and that was seeing and saying goodbye to my love one last time.

I went to my love's wake six days after her death. I requested that my time with her be alone, as friends and family would have the last two hours to themselves. A few hours before, I had picked up Karey's parents from the airport. It was the first time we met. Our whole relationship was over the telephone, but you would've swore we saw each other everyday by the way we embraced each other.

They were going to stay at my place until they left. I treated them to the fish market downtown on Harbor. Over King Crab Legs and Lobster, we talked about some of everything, from their marriage of 25 plus years, to my recent book. However, as I was starting to explain the circumstances around their daughter's death, her mom stopped me and said some words that would forever change my life.

"T.J. Young man. We did not come to talk about the bad of her life. We came to talk about the good. Death is only the beginning, for our journey does not stop because we leave this shell. Life is everlasting, and we are energy. We dissipate from one and transform into another. I am here to celebrate with you, my husband, some family and her friends. I love you like a son, but I will not allow you to feel sorry for yourself about what happened. Now, we will eat dinner and laugh and rejoice."

All I could do was look at her with amazement. This had to be the Superwoman of Superwomen. Her daughter was dead, yet all she could concentrate on was making sure her life was celebrated to the upmost. Now, I really regretted not marrying Karey. I could tell that I would've been part of a great family.

As I walked in to the funeral home, I looked for the signs for where my beautiful queen would be showcased one final time. I came upon two double doors, with the letters inside the glass saying: Karey D. Taylor. I took a few deep breaths as I constantly repeated her name time after time inside of my head. This is it I thought. The last time I would be alone with my love. I looked up to the sky, saying a silent prayer to God to not let me break down in this parlor. I hope he heard me, seeing that I was cursing him out not to long ago.

I opened both doors and just stood in the doorway. I stood in the doorway. I stood in the doorway. It seems like I stood there forever. I gazed down at her open casket. The tears began to flow, as memories of our first meeting started to fly through my brain. I collected myself eventually and started my journey. I paced my walk down to her casket slowly, wanting to take in everything in this setting. I was very observant. I wanted each light to work. Every pew was to be polished. Hell, if roses were being used to decorate this place, I was making sure they were in proper position. If my baby was going to be sent off, she was going to be sent off in a proper fashion. There would be no screw ups, or else the funeral director's family might be up here looking at them. I finally made it to the casket. Immediately, the tears began to flow. All I could do was cry as I noticed she was laid to rest in the same red dress I had first met her in. She looked so peaceful. It really looked like she was sleep, and all she needed was a kiss for me to wake her up. I rubbed my hand across her head and gave her one last kiss on her forehead.

"I love you beautiful," I whispered to her. I pulled out an envelope from my pocket that contained a poem that I wrote her. The words said:

"I think about the day when I first saw your face, young and full of life, I didn't know back then you would be my wife, I just thought you were another one of those girls, over time, feelings became enveloped, thoughts became more seductive and I became more of a productive man in our relationship, taking trips every week it seemed, running around as if our lives would never end, and then...our lives really began,

the exchange of an I love you eventually turned into an I Do, and I did you like no man had ever done before, from the floor, bed or in the kitchen, I had you as my late night snack and early morning breakfast, you on the other hand brought the bitch side out of this man, cause you sucked me so good that I almost bought your old man before me some Jordan's, and you rode me so good that I thought your were part horse, when you nothing more that part freak..time passed and kids came, they grew up and we grew old, our bones would soon start to go brittle and things that seemed so little became huge tasks...see even though our youthfulness didn't last, you could never tell, because our love grew with each passing day, and when we finally became old and gray, our interaction was more intimate than anytime we were busy sucking, licking and swallowing each other, holding hands as I look at what you created as a mother,

and what they produced once they got grown, it seemed like grandkids in the home was more fun than our original kids, and me telling my grand boys about the things that I once did would remain a secret to your ears, because I had to let them know how gramps got down before I met you, see the day is gonna come for us all when rocking chairs and smiles is our only choice, so while we're young, make that woman moist and kiss her like there's no tomorrow...because we don't know if we will even see tomorrow"

I wrote it based on us being old and looking back at our lives as a couple. I imagined us having three or four children and just living the good life that all married couples should live. I thought about sitting with her on the porch in rocking chairs, talking about all the great memories that we had. Now, all those could have beens were just a memory. As I gave her one last look, I did the one thing that I should've done sooner. I pulled out a black box. Inside, was a 3 carat diamond ring. It had three 2 carat stones up top and five 1 carat stones on each side of the band. I slid it on her finger, and balled tears as I apologized for not doing this sooner. Now, I would never have the chance. I would see her one last time tomorrow. I kissed her forehead and walked out the funeral parlor. I didn't look back.

At the funeral, there was a wide range of emotions. Her mother stayed strong. A stone, yet somber look on her face, as she wanted no one doing anything but celebrating her daughter's life. Her husband, from the looks of it, reflected all of her strength into himself. You could tell he was down and out. His wife strength allowed him no more than teary eyes, as he tried to keep it together. As for everyone else, there was nothing but tears flowing. A lot of her college friends were here. There was so much emotion in this room you would've thought we were at a Maury show taping.

This however was amazing. To see how many lives Karey touched truly brought me joy to call myself her other half. Everyone embraced each other as we reflected on Karey's great life. San Diego State reps even showed up to deliver her parents a framed Bachelor's Degree in Communications that she would've earned. I honestly thought that was a heartfelt thing to do. After the opening prayer, acknowledgements and every other thing associated with a funeral was complete, I was asked to come up and say some words on behalf of my love. I started off explaining how we met, and how we had bonded over time, eventually falling in love. My biggest speech was to come though.

"So for y'all who didn't notice, A ring was on Karey's finger. I placed it there last night, as I did have on plans to marry her and have her as my lifelong partner. To Mr. and Mrs. Taylor, I apologize for not doing it sooner."

As the tears began to flow from myself and the rest of the crowd, I saved my absolute best tribute for last.

"I wrote Karey this poem. Bare with me please." With tears in my ears, and a cracked voice, I began to read:

"My best friend is more than someone I share my deepest darkest secrets with, its the one who can replace my heart with theirs if mines ever stops beating, in my case, my best friend comes with a slim waist, gorgeous face, billion dollar smile and a stomach that I can iron my dreams up on, but this isn't why she my best friend, its cause she's the one who in the end, will be my crutch,

see I never thought of it as such, until she told me, saying that our bond wasn't the definition of society, and I sat back and thought, she's right, cause I have found myself getting up at all kinds of odd hours in the night, just to answer a text or a call from her, see for her, I don't mind this, cause it could be to blow a kiss thru the phone, or her calling for me to ease her fears, after having a nightmare that a man was at her car, see what she didn't know, was that after we had that talk, I went back to sleep, jumped into her nightmare and cold clocked the same dude who was at her window stalking, I put her in my arms and started walking her to her house, put her in her bed, gave her a kiss on her forehead, and stayed there until she had fallen asleep, what happened to the car you ask, nothing, but it was part of her traumatic experience that I was considerate enough to leave it there for the night,

see it still amazes me that a conversation on a random night led to where me and my best friend are at today, hell, my best friend even got the best treatment in the world one day, she got me sprung with no springs, only if she knew I sing Tank songs at random times of the day, that's just the playfulness I got with my best friend, cause in the end, I need to give her laughter to sometimes ease her mind from what life is throwing at her, yet when it throws something at her, it always strikes me, cause its like she is a literal piece of me, yet she is so far, far away, not a day goes by that she isn't soaked into my thinking cap, even when I take naps, I get a quick visual of her laying next to me, *and I wake up feeling refreshed, see I got a few best friends, but she's the best of the best, matter fact, I've written her so much poetry from the heart, that if you took an X-ray of my chest, you'd see it bleeds blue and black ink, see my best friend, I call her Queen, but I gotta find something higher than that, cause my best friend is even worthy of a better title than that, but shhh, don't tell my best friend that I wrote her this, just know, that this is a kiss, sent to her, in a poetic fashion."*

The crowd went silent and you could hear rat piss on cotton. Then, a huge applause let out. Karey always knew, but now the world knew exactly how I felt about my true love. As the crowd filed out, we had one last send off for my love. Since her body was to be immediately flown to Alabama for burial, everyone inside met at Fiesta Island. This was Karey's favorite spot in the city. It was her reflect on life spot. She would call me sometimes after she drove out there and we'd talk for hours on end. We all had red and black balloons, the colors of San Diego State.

"To Karey!!!!! May you live forever in our hearts!!!" Her mother said these words with a sharpness that would've cut the air if that was possible. We all let our balloons go in the air as a final goodbye to my love. I broke down immediately afterwards, but like always, Mark was there by my side to give me encouragement and let me know that it will be okay. My love was not dead. She would forever live through me and any and all accomplishments I achieved from this point on. Good bye my love. I love you.

CHAPTER 10

That night after the funeral I had a dream. I was walking down a barren street with old, beat up homes. It was damn near like walking through the Harbor section of East Chicago. Everything was so desolate and dry. There was no signs of life, and the sky was the ugliest brown I have ever seen. It literally looked like someone took a huge crap in the clouds.

It was extremely cold outside, even though there was no signs of snow, and no wind gusts. All of a sudden, everything just broke. The sky turned blue. The homes became very beautiful and this bright light just appeared out of nowhere. I stopped walking as I was mesmerized by this light. It was burning right in front of me, but I didn't feel any heat or anything like that coming off of it. Out of the blue, a beautiful, white robed figure walked out.

"Karey!!," I screamed. It was her. She stopped and just smiled. I walked up to her and just stared in amazement at her beauty. She was beautiful in the physical, but all of a sudden she was a beautiful that I couldn't even describe.

"I love you T.J. You will find another me."

Wait, what the hell did that mean??? She slowly started to back away. **"Karey!!!,"** I yelled, but all she did was smile and back away. I tried to walk up to her, but I was stuck and couldn't move my body one inch. Suddenly, everything burst into flames and I shot up in my bed. I woke up in a cold sweat.

Quick, panting breaths were all I could get out. I looked around my room for any sign of life. Nothing. I kept trying to tell myself that it was real. However, I knew it was just a dream. It was comforting to know that my love was in a better place, but it sucked that I wouldn't be able to see her here in my presence again. But her telling me I will find another her. What the hell did that mean???

I didn't want another her. All I wanted was her. She was gone. There was no one who could take her place. Not nann women on this earth could even match her in my eyes. Irreplaceable is what I thought, regardless of what she told me. A new beginning maybe? I think that's what the fire represented. I thought of that story of the phoenix rising from the ashes. Maybe this was my moment to rise from the ashes. I cried my eyes out. Just earlier today, I attended my love's home going celebration. That was the hardest thing that I ever had to deal with. How would I continue on living life without my true love? This wasn't the puppy love crap I had in high school. This was indeed the real thing. Just then, I noticed one of the drawers partially opened. I got up in my moonlit room to close it, until I noticed what was in it. it was my 9mm Beretta. I just stared at it. I pulled the whole drawer open to expose its whole body along with its insides sitting off to the side. I grabbed that bitch, one of the clips and walked back to the edge of my bed. I slowly analyzed both objects in my hands as I thought about my whole life. From the rough streets of East Chi I survived the gun.

Now, I embraced its power to take life as I studied it. I slowly inserted the clip into her and pulled the slide back to chamber a round. The clicking sound never sounded so good. I took the safety off. I slowly got up and walked over towards the mirror. I stared at myself, as for the first time in my life I did not recognize my own self. I thought to the first time I met Karey at my first book signing. I thought about how our eyes caught contact and how her beautiful smile lit up my soul. The tears began to flow as I thought back to all our love making sessions. How she would tell me to make her feel like the only woman alive.

At this point, my eyes were red and my face was soaked. I put the gun barrel right beneath my chin. As I closed my eyes and imagined what life would be like if I ended it all. Just then, a vision arose in my head.

"Daddy," a beautiful lil girl shouted out. **"Daddy, no!!!"** *POP!!!!*

I came back too. I clutched the gun with both hands and sat it down. I realized in that moment that I had to finish out this dream not only for myself, but for all who looked to me in tough times, including my dead love and unborn daughter. I don't know why that drawer was open. I don't know if it was the devil trying to tell me to end it all, or was it God testing me out. Either way, I am just glad that I didn't pull that trigger.

***

Weeks had now passed and I was back to my normal self for the most part. There were times that I broke-down, but I had continued on with life as usual. I had been back in contact with my fam from back at the crib and the team was ready for the next mission. Mr. Johnson called me on some how are you doing type stuff, and we had a very meaningful conversation. He thanked me for giving him the opportunity to work with me. That was kind of ironic, as I should have been the one thanking him. He was the one who took a chance on me.

I met with my team one day, as I planned on dropping a bombshell on them for my next project. I had written stories for quite a while and made a killing doing it, whether it was in high school or professionally. Now, I was ready to shift gears to see if I could leave my mark in another industry. With Mark, my accountant and other members of my marketing team in the room, I gave them the news.

"Team, I want to take a break from writing and delve into the word of slam poetry." The room was silent and full of blank stares.

"Muthafucka have you been drinkin??!!!," Mark exclaimed.

"I know yo ass done been drinking some shit."

"Naw bruh," I told him. "I'm dead serious."

"Can everyone leave the room please?," Mark said in a stern voice. Everyone did, as me and him had a solo conversation. This dude was a close personal friend of mine, and I know he would tell me exactly how he felt.

"T, I know its been hard losing your lady and your child. But man, you got something going great. And now you gone give it all up to try and be a poet?" I stared at him for a long minute which seemed like eternity.

"Yea." He just looked at me. He stared and took a deep breath. He stepped back, looked me up and down and said,

"Lets do it."

I couldn't believe it. I thought this dude was gonna cuss me out or tell me that we needed to hit the strip club to straighten my mind out or something. He was very supportive to my surprise.

"T, let me tell you something bruh. Even though you're young, you make grown man decisions. I may be 6 years your senior, but one thing I will never do is tell a man to not pursue a dream that they want to pursue. You've accomplished much at your young age, and I have full confidence that whatever you delve yourself into, you will be successful. So brotha, lets do this if you really believe you can wreck this market."

I couldn't believe this. To have the support of this man meant a lot. I called my team back in the room, arranged for when we would meet next, and me and Mark left out together and headed towards Red Lobster to celebrate this new beginning in my life. What better way to celebrate than to mangle some cheddar biscuits. I just hope this brother didn't smash em all before I got a chance to get some. He was heavy set and could eat. I had to get em while the getting was good.

***

Finally, a poetry slam had arrived in San Diego for me to showcase my skills. I wasn't so much concentrated on winning, but I was concentrated on leaving a lasting impression where no one would forget who I was. I entered the student hall down at UCSD where the event was being held. My God I yelled in my head. It was more chocolate in here than a Hershey's factory. All these women looked around my age.

Damn, I had been in San Diego for some time, and had never seen none of these girls. Maybe it was because I was concentrated so much on my relationship that I didn't even notice other women. However, I was noticing now, even if it was because of some tragic circumstances. I signed my name up on the list as a slam competitor and patiently waited my turn.

Ten poets in all would compete, with the audience acting as judges. The host approached me and informed me that I would be going seventh. As each competitor went up, I analyzed them carefully. I noticed how they projected their voice, how they altered their voice tones, their hand movements, so on and so forth. The whole time I was observing, I was thinking one thing inside of my head. *WHICH ONE OF THESE MOTHER FUCKERS ARE COMING IN SECOND PLACE????*

Finally, it was my time to go. I walked up to the stage, took a quick glance and jumped off my three minute piece with the opening line:

"I wanna give you that type of love that makes your orgasms have orgasms." Screams started coming from the crowd, and I knew it was time to go in. I went in line after line until I just finished under the three minute mark. The crowd went wild, and I thought I was set up for victory. I scored a 9.8 out of ten with the crowd, which was the highest score of the night so far. I was humbled, but I knew there were three more competitors left, and crowds lean from artist to artist in this craft. Finally, the last poet went, and it was time to tally up all the scores. My heart was pounding. I had the highest vote from the crowd, but I know strange things can happen. Finally, they announced the results.

"And the winner of tonight's poetry slam, and headed to the regional competition in L.A. is..Mr. T.J. Washington!!! Betta known as 20 Stax!!!!"

The crowd erupted in a thunderous ovation. I couldn't believe it. My first ever poetry slam, and I killed it!!! From the front, as I went to accept my small trophy, I could see Mark in the crowd, way in the back, pumping his fist. I didn't even know he was coming, but it was good to see him there. His support really meant a lot to me. As the crowd started to disperse, I shook many hands, got several congrats and Mark finally made his way through the crowd. he greeted me with a big ass hug.

"MY DUDE!! MY DUDE!!! YOU DID IT!!!" Man, this guy was more excited than I was. I was happy, but still trying to sink this feeling in. All I concentrated on right now was one thing. I was going to go to the City of Angels and be a devil. The time was here and my time was now. This couldn't have come at a better time. After all I had went through with the loss of my woman, I felt I had did her proud.

CHAPTER 11

I went to bed that night, but ironically, I didn't feel like a winner. I ran down the list of things that I had accomplished. Survived East Chicago, check. Survived Southern California, check. Established myself as an author, check. Won a poetry competition, which I really didn't give a damn about cause I personally think its full of 98% frauds for the most part, check.

I did all that, yet I felt something was missing. This did not have anything at all to do with my two favorite girls dying. This ran a lot deeper than what most people thought. I laid in the bed and thought about all the decisions I made in life. Even though a lot of good had come out of those situations, I felt like I settled for a lot. I felt like I just accepted some things to accept them and hoped for the best to come out of the situation. Contrary to what most believe, my life revolved around more than just writing books. There were the nights on the road where I just felt lonely in a hotel room, even though I had someone to come home too. Karey never gave me reason to doubt her in anyway, but my perfect person may never repeat themselves. She kissed me how I liked. She sexed me how I liked. She wasn't a timid girl. We loved the same things. We shared the same expressions. The word no didn't exist with us. However, I was scared that the ones I would meet from here on out would have scars and the word no etched so deep into their mind that I would take the fall for any and everything.

I didn't want to pay for another mans mistakes, nor did I just want to settle for any ol girl. Contrary to what people believe, it takes more than love to make a relationship last. These were the 2000's, and I didn't want to meet the next woman who was stuck in the 1950's. I also thought about how even though I have the big house, the money and friends, I missed my mom dearly. We talked everyday, but it still wasn't the same. She had it hard after my pops died. Even though he was a business owner, she was so nervous about messing up everything he left for us, that she moved from the Illinois suburbs to East Chicago.

She didn't want to lose the big house, the cars, none of that. She traded the luxurious life for the simple life. Yea, my hood had its share of problems, but it wasn't the worst place to grow up in. I needed to see her more than anything. I gave Mark a call and told him that I would be gone for a few days. I was heading back to East Chicago for a much needed vacation. I needed to get back to my roots to remind myself of who I truly was.

As soon as the plane touched down, my mom was there to greet me at baggage claim.

"Babyyyyyyyyyyy!!!!!!!" She said that emphatically as she gave me a death grip of a hug.

"Hey mom," I barreled out with a few tears coming out of my eyes. It had been two years since I seen her, and I was going to make this time count. We talked about everything once we hit the car. I informed her on what she didn't know was going on in my life, to just some of the things that I were planning.

This was a great feeling. Me and my mom, sitting and talking in the car as we always did when I was younger. Back then, it was the talks of what did I want to do when I got older. Now, they were talks of what more am I going to do. This was truly a great experience. Just a few minutes from the house, she stopped at my favorite eat spot. J&J's Fish and Chicken was the bomb around here.

I stopped in and scooped me up a six piece wing dinner with white bread and coleslaw. After that, I told moms to swing by White Castle's and let me get a nine piece chicken ring.

"Dang fat bo!!! You wanna save some food for the homeless?"

Moms didn't understand though. It had been so long since I had been home, and I wanted to savor everything about this experience. This was more than just a vacation. This was a physical and mental getaway that not even the most expensive trip could top.

***

I laid in my childhood room that night, looking around at the walls. My mom had left my room just the way it was. Dusty posters of Stephon Marbury, Kobe Bryant and MJ littered my walls. Flyers from old parties and imitation rap plaques covered up the remaining spaces. Heck, I even had an old blue demon mask hanging up that I had made in ceramics class my junior year of high school.

Old memories started to sink in, and all of a sudden found myself reliving everything that I once did. Contrary to how some people act, not everything that happened in your past was a bad thing. Some things you want to happen again. Some moments you wanted to relive. I knew just what to do at this moment. It wasn't a guarantee, but I was going to give it a try. I scrolled through my phone and found the number I was looking for. The phone rang four times before I was ready to just hang up. All of a sudden, I heard the sweetest voice say Hello.

"Ashley, is this Ashley?"

"Ummmm, yea. who is this?"

"IT'S POT LIQUOR BABY!!" It took her a minute to let those words sink in, but once she did, she bellowed out the loudest T.J. you could ever imagine. My goodness, we must have talked for a good three hours. She was still downstate in school, but she would be home this weekend, which gave me less than 24 hours to prep, seeing that it was a chill Thursday night. I was so excited, but I had to contain myself. I asked her did she want to get out when she got back, and she happily obliged. Oh boy, I could see this trip already turning into something great.

Ashley arrived home early Friday afternoon. I gave her time to get settled in with her family and chill. They had a four day weekend down at her school, so she wouldn't be back on the road until Monday. Around two o'clock on that Friday, she hit me up.

"My mama said bring yo tail over here to get some of this macaroni."

Woooooooooooooooo is all I could say in my head, going into my Ric Flair mode. Her mom made some bomb Mac-n-cheese, and it wasn't one of those if you were hungry type of things. When she made a pan, you ate. No questions asked. I arrived to her house and was greeted with a huge hug from Ashley. We walked on in and met her mama in the kitchen, who was indulging in a plate of her own.

"Hey boy!!! Sit yo tail down and eat some of this food." Haha. That was Ms. Carter for you. Always in a good mood and always made you feel welcome. We chopped it up on a funny tip before me and Ash decided to dip out. We headed to the store to get some ice cream. She always had a thing for some strawberry ice cream. We copped it and went back to the house to chill in her basement room and watch movies.

As the hours drifted slowly past midnight, we found our talks getting deeper and deeper, as we were getting sleepier and sleepier. At about one in the morning, in her basement room, with her head firmly on my shoulder, she looked up at me and asked a question.

"T.J. Did you mean it that day some years back when you told me that you loved me?"

I calmly leaned my head back to look in her eyes. "Yes I did"

She smiled. Then, she slowly got up to lock her door. Everyone in the house was knocked out at this point, and the only light we had on was coming from the TV. She crawled back into bed, climbed on top of me and told me in the softest voice

"Then come get what's yours." We slowly took each other clothes off, as tongues got to flipping in and out of each other's mouths. Once fully naked, I slowly laid her down and began to lick her love box nice and slow. She tasted like Honey Nut Cheerios. If I could, I would stay down here forever. I didn't want anything done for me I thought, as I climbed back up after making her legs shake. I slowly slid inside of her and we began to make slow passionate love.

This was my Karey before Karey, even though we had never dated. We stayed as quiet as possible, which I think made it more intriguing. As I hit her from the back, she had no choice but to put her face in the pillow and scream. I was going to town on this kuda snap. Finally, after what seemed like forever, I cut loose on that flat, sexy stomach of hers. We just looked at each other. Sweaty, exhausted and worn out on both ends, I laid on top of her, kissed her and we exchanged I love you's back and forth.

Eventually, I got up, got a rag and wipe ourselves clean of cum. Shower though? Naw, neither one of us were thinking that. We ended up laying there on some wet sheets, holding each other until we drifted off into dreamland. There were women, and then there was Ashley. It is definitely true what they say. You will never forget your first love. Indeed, I did not.

CHAPTER 12

It had now been a few months since I went back to the crib. A lot had happened over that time. I finished 4th in the regionals in L.A. for the spoken word competition, yet I kept progressing in that craft, even though I hadn't participated in any slams since then. Another book of mines that I finished prior to taking a break had been published and hit The New York Times best sellers list. I was in the driver's seat controlling my own destiny. Not to mention that I had also turned 21 in the process. Damn.

August 17th, 2003 seemed like yesterday. Now, it was well into 2005 and I was living the life. One random night, I decided to hit the streets to see what I could get into. I wasn't looking for anything special. I just wanted to kick back and enjoy myself for a little bit. I stumbled across a club called the 94. In San Diego, this was a black man's paradise. It was a good mix of young and old on the age and music tip. There was hardly any drama associated with this place, unless drama involved standing in a long line waiting to get in. That's why I brought my black tail in that joint during happy hour. The first time I ever came here, I thought I was Mr. GQ. Popped up to the joint at 8:30 and didn't get in until 11. Happy hour was free of charge, plus I was a popcorn junkie, so the fact that had free popcorn made it worth it to come in so early.

I seen a few of my regular partners from around the city in there, and we just made it happen. Tre, Sin, Troy, Anthony, all my real homies away from the people I met through the writing industry. The women were nice and the vibe was tight. Man, you couldn't ask for a better kickback then this. Around 12:30 I rolled out. I hopped in my car and jetted out the parking lot towards Jack in the Box. On the West, they called it Jack in the Crack, and it was the ideal food after you left the club. I pulled up to the drive thru and ordered two supreme croissant sandwiches. As I scooped it up from the window, I pulled out, did a quick check to make sure they had my joint right and hauled ass towards the 15 freeway.

***

I was now back on the scene, getting ready for my next promo tour. Over time, my presentations were less about my books, and more towards young entrepreneurship. I had quite a list for this tour. Oakland, California. Fairfield, California. Richmond, California. Seattle, Washington. Vancouver, British Columbia. Las Vegas, Nevada. Phoenix, Arizona. The final wrap up city would be down in Longview, Texas. I had rocked in the Bay Area and Vegas several times before, but the rest of these joints were foreign to me. This would be great though. As always, I was hoping to be a major influence to my peers so they could become young entrepreneurs, especially my black peeps. I shut the Bay Area down and headed up to Seattle. Rain, rain, rain was all I seen. Inside U of W, pretty women were all I seen. Unlike the school nickname of Huskies, all the women were built like stallions. After that, I kicked things off in Vancouver, and boy oh boy, this would be the place I would never forget.

This was much different than any other place in the states. First off, weed was legal up here. Now, I never was a smoker, but seeing it smoked freely up here was quite tempting. As usual, Mark was by my side and even he started to get tense about this situation.

"Man, these niggas gone have me blowing big." All I could think was here we go. I knew my mans. That was the sign that before we left, he was going to blow big. We had two days before another event, so we decided to kick back and cut loose. We took in all the sights and sounds that Vancouver had to offer. The food was great, the people were chill and these Canadian women were ooo wee.

This was my first time traveling to Canada, but from the looks of it, it damn sure wouldn't be the last. We hit up this club called Atlantis and hot damn!!! The minute we walked in, we could tell that this would be a great night. Our hotel was down the street, so we didn't have to worry bout driving. With that, we immediately hit the bar. We ordered our typical medication of

Hennessey and Coke, and started vibing. Man, I couldn't believe how beautiful these women were up here. American women didn't have a damn thing on them. We were all dancing, all having a good time, and me and Mark were drunk as hell. As the night progressed, we started to chop it up with these three local ladies who were feeling us. I don't know about Mark, but my liquor vision told me that these broads were on point. We scampered away from the club with the ladies and jumped in a SUV. As one of the loves I'll just call Juanita was driving, Mark was tore up in the back screaming

"I'm hot!!! Baby I'm hot!!!"

"How hot are you daddy?," said the one I'll call Gee Gee.

"Girlllllllll. I'm so hot, that when I want chicken, the chicken plucks off his feathers and hops in the grease nigga!!!! Cluck Cluck bitch!!!"

We all started dying laughing, as we knew this dude was faded beyond belief. We arrived at a house in a neighborhood that looked descent, but what could I tell, seeing that my vision was seriously impaired. We set up shop in the living room with these three lovelies and started to blaze up.

Damn, I'm not a weed expert by any means, but this shit hit off like some straight killa!!! One puff had me feeling like I was tap dancing on the Disney Channel with Mickey Mouse rapping. We blazed, talked and drank until the wee hours of the morning, until Juanita and Gee-Gee started kissing each other. This other chick, who I'll just call Never Again came up on me and started kissing me on my neck. Shoot, I already knew what time it was. The lights went dim and it was on.

The next afternoon I was groggy in rolling over. My arm was asleep and I had no recollection of the whole night. I remember being in the club and coming to a house with some girl, and that was it. Right then, my arm felt dead and I heard a loud snore. I turned my head to see this fat, greasy, salt pork cut of a woman lying on my arm knocked out. *OMG* I thought. *I know damn well I didn't get my rocks off on this.* After corralling her hefty sized self off my arm, I looked up to see Mark smiling, yet shaking his head in disgust.

"Glad you on the team playa," he told me. "If it was me, you would've just gone ass less."

I looked at him, looked at her and just wanted to scream. I had stroked this fat girl to unconsciousness.

"What happened with you mane?," I asked Mark.

"Shidddd. I knocked 'em both off. Mother and daughter combo." I looked at him and was jealous as hell. This lucky mofo got two bad ones. A mother and daughter at that!!! Me however, I got stuck with Shamu.

"T, you ever got yo balls and yo ass licked at the same time???" Right then and there, I knew it was time to go. However, since the deed had already been done, I waited around until they all were up so they could cook us some breakfast. That's the least they could do for us delivering them some dick. Pancakes, grits, sausage and ham quickly made me forget about slaying the morbidly obese beast.

***

The event wrapped up a few days later, and we followed up Vancouver by killing it in Vegas, Phoenix and Longview over the next two weeks. We were now back in Daygo and the checks were in the bank. At home, I took the time to ensure my fam in Chi and SD was good. I peeled out one day to just enjoy some time by myself. I hit Huffman's up on Euclid and Imperial for some chitlins. It was funny. The area where I had my scariest moment in Daygo, I was now back. This time though, no one was trying to kill me. I then stopped through FAMMART; the local swap meet and copped me some fitted caps and some dirt cheap jeans.

Lastly, I swung downtown to meet up with a buddy O-Dog. He had gotten out the service and opened up a smooth Neo Soul spot called The Don. We began talking on how to spread a musical and spoken word movement away from downtown, and expand it into the neighboring counties. The meeting was productive and lasted about an hour and a half. Good ideas and good food here at this Japanese joint made things great. Our plan was going to be executed real soon. We parted ways and went on about our business.

I hit the freeway at about 9 p.m., heading home for the evening. Along the way, I decided to stop off in Mira Mesa and holla at my cousin. He always stayed up late and was never in bed before 12. I got to the house and everything looked normal. His car was in the driveway, porch lights were on, but no one was answering the door. Suddenly, I grabbed the door knob to see the door was unlocked. Before I even though about entering, I went to my car and grabbed my bitch, just in case someone would have to catch lead.

"CUZ," I yelled. "CUZ, YOU IN HERE!!!" I still didn't

get a response. Just as I rounded the corner, I could see two feet poking out of the bedroom.

"**CUZ!!!**" I ran up to him, but it wasn't him. It was some guy I had never seen. He was dead. *What the hell* was all I could think. Who was this guy, and what was he doing in cuz house? Just then, I heard police sirens. Hot damn. I was in deep shit again I thought.

CHAPTER 13

I heard as the police pulled up to the house somebody must've seen me enter the house or something. **"HELP!!!"** I shouted out as I heard them exit their cruisers. **"HELP, HELP!!!,"** I kept repeating myself. I even took the clip out of my nine, un-chambered the solo round and slid it off to the side. I wasn't even trying to risk getting shot up. Hell, a black man would get shot 50 times for just going to the strip club.

"WHERE ARE YOU???!!!," I heard one of the officers beckon.

"I'M BACK HERE!!! UNARMED!!! NEXT TO A DEAD BODY!!! I'M ON THE GROUND!!!" I wasn't taking any chances. I stayed face down as I heard the officer come in the room. He called over the radio to report there was a stiff, along with a possible suspect. Other officers soon followed and I was cuffed and taken outside. As they took me outside, I could see a crowd of neighbors gathered near the house, looking to see what was going on. They sat me on the curb and started to ask me questions. I explained to them the whole story about how the door was unlocked, to how I grabbed my pistol and went inside to check on my cousin.

Just then, my cousin's neighbor Vince began talking to the police. He told them I used to stay there and that I caused no trouble. Still, the police had to be cautious, seeing that I was found next to a dead body.

"Is that your cousin?," one of the officers beckoned.

"No sir. I have no clue who that is. I have my cousin's number if you would like it?" As forensics and what seemed like the whole crew of NCSI descended in and out of the house, the police finally got a hold of my cousin. He was on vacation in Texas visiting his daughter and grand children. He confirmed who I was and that I was a former resident. Their conversation continued over the phone as the body was wheeled out. As the phone conversation ended, he advised me that I would have to be brought down to the station for further questioning.

I was brought down to headquarters. Now, I knew what those cats you seen in the movies felt like. I told them step by step what happened, never changing my story. There were no worries about my gun, as I had all the proper paperwork. After an hour long conversation, I thought I was going home, but I was told to wait. A few minutes later, detectives came back and let me know who the dead man was. It was my cousin's son. They found the back window of the house broken open, and he died of a drug overdose. All I could think about now was the many folks I seen coming up who lost their lives because of a needle. That bertha was a bitch. That's what they called it in the land. Every man who went up against her ended up taking an L. She stayed undefeated with millions of permanent knockouts under her belt.

***

Weeks passed and everything was back to normal. I had taken a spur of the moment cruise to Hawaii during that time to indulge in the island life for a little while. That was great. All I have to say is if any of you haven't been, and you do plan on going, it is a must that you hit up Dukes on the Waikiki strip. It truly is the best place on earth. Zanzibar's was also a hot spot down in Honolulu. Lord knows the women in that joint were top notch. Besides that, I was on my grind as usual. You would think with all my success, that I would just sit back and enjoy my riches. Not this guy. I was rich, but I continued to work as if I didn't have two nickels to rub together.

On my way to the top, I remembered two brothers I had met along the way. Both were fashion designers and I wanted to partner up with them so I could give them some much needed exposure for their brands. It was always good to see black men strive for the top to beat out the stereotype that unfortunately plagues us. With a few meetings, all I's were dotted and T's were crossed. I would ensure that whenever I gave a seminar to a young crowd, I would be rocking Lapaix and F.L.A.V.A.

Me and O-Dog organized an event with the city of San Diego on public speaking and becoming an entrepreneur. This would be a huge hit, as we could continue to use our strengths to help others. We were able to rent out the Convention Center and sell it out in less than 24 hours. What really made this special was that this would be the first time someone shared the stage with me.

O had been prosperous in his own right, and he deserved this moment just as well as me. After a dramatic 30 minute presentation about business ownership in which he nailed it harder than Clinton did females, it was my turn to get the crowd going. Feeding off the energy O left, I kept it going and in the end, the crowd was going nuts. We both spent the next hour after our presentations greeting the crowd, collecting business cards and just basking in the moment. As I went out to the hall to get me a drink, a young lady came up to me from behind.

"My goodness, I really loved your speech. You just gave me all the motivation in the world to achieve what I want to in life."

That was humbling to hear, and after a small conversation, I dismissed myself until she grabbed my arm. I gave her that black folks look like what the hell are you doing.

"I'm so sorry. Would you like to go out for some drinks?"

"No ma'am. Have a good night." I walked away thinking nothing of it. I mean, I had been used to women throwing themselves at me from city to city. This seemed like the same situation, and I didn't have time to deal with the drama. I was well established, young and fly. The last thing I wanted to do was to get caught up with some random woman. After me and O left, we headed to Mission Valley to enjoy a good steak and we went home.

The next morning, my doorbell started ringing like crazy. I

was still in bed. I looked over to the clock to see that it was 6:56 in the morning. I tried to ignore it, but whoever the S.O.B. that was ringing it wasn't stopping. I got up pissed, still groggy and I got even more upset when I stubbed my right baby toe against the bed post trying to slide my foot in one of my house shoes. I finally got down the stairs to my door. ***Ding Dong***

"HOLD ON!!!" I was pissed off. I yanked open the door. Low and behold, it was the woman from last night's event.

"Excuse me. What are you doing at my house?" At first, I was hoping that I was dreaming and that I would wake up real soon. However, I wasn't.

"I was just so intrigued from your words last night that I had to talk to you on a more personal level." Right then and there I had to stop her.

"Look miss, I'm flattered that my words influenced you, but you popping up at my door like this is rude and borderline psycho. You need to leave before I call the cops." She gave me a distraught but kind of sinister look.

"Did you just call me psycho?"

"Yes I did. Now, could you please leave before I call the cops?" With her eyes watering, she frowned up her face and said "Ok." I made sure to watch from my door until she left. However, before she opened her car door, she took one last look at me and said

"We will be talking later."

She sped off and I walked out to the street to make sure this crazy bitch was gone. I don't like calling women crazy, nor do I like calling them bitches. In this case, it was very much warranted. I left it alone after that and went back in the house. Since I was now up, I said screw it and cooked me some grits and shrimp. What y'all know about that country grub? I may have been from East Chicago, but all my family was deep rooted from the back woods of Alabama. I decided to just spend this day in the house. I used this day not only to wind down from last night, but to catch up with all of my family.

I called as many of my family members as possible. Everyone form Chicago, Indiana, Alabama and Michigan was doing good to say the least. My cousin Eddie T. in Detroit was still on his usual. He was smoking weed, working and banging the backs out of women. That's what he did. I winded down the night watching the news and Coming to America. I waltzed upstairs finally around one in the morning, and drifted off to dreamland. An hour or so into my sleep, I heard a loud bang at my door and tires screech. Fuck the 9; I grabbed the shotgun. Whoever this was, they were about to meet Jesus.

I slowly maneuvered around the house, not seeing anyone or anything out of place. Still cautious, I opened the front door and saw a wrapped package. I was skeptical as all hell. Slowly, I opened it up and found some Jordan's in a box. They were a size 12. They were too small for me since I wore a 15. Inside, I found a note. I love you, Sharee. Ahh shit, I now was dealing with a crazy, psycho ass bitch

CHAPTER 14

I could not believe this. This was some straight stalker mess. I wasn't going to call the police this late. I would simply take this to the local police department in the morning, and make a report about being harassed. Luckily, she was at the convention, so maybe she was caught on a few cameras. I was really hoping that a camera caught our small conversation so that the police could identify her properly.

As I took the box upstairs, I saw a long envelope underneath the shoes. I can't front. She might have been crazy, but the girl did have good taste in shoes. I took the envelope and opened it up. Hell, I figured since I'm already up, I might as well see what other BS she wrote me. It was a poem entitled Sharee: The reconstruction of a woman's heart. It read:

She came lookin to be rebuilt from her past relationships, men who had built walls around her heart for the sole purpose to tear her apart inside, and no one would ever notice this hidden pain, see it pained me that she had to endure this, because to her, a kiss no longer symbolized sealing a bond, it told her that lips lie, even when they come together, so when I met her, she channeled her soul to mine with no satellites, or remote controls,

it was just my sole job to control her emotions until she was fully tuned in to me, it was a struggle to get Sharee, cause when she saw me, she saw every other man that laid out the blueprint plans to construct her destruction, so it was more like demolition, a dick and layin of some pipe was what caused her explosion, but in the midst of that explosion, she was buried under her own rubble, cause once something is demolished, like any construction worker, they leave it behind for the next man to clean up,

see she was fed up, so she stayed down, even though she knew to look up, and once she did, she saw me, thinkin I was a clone of the next guy, she started to sigh at the thought of opening her heart again, so I told her to keep it closed, let me stock your store with groceries and produce, so I may produce to you a different fruit that you have yet to taste, because I see in your past that haste turned to waste, so Im a pace this walk right here with you, I wont address you as boo, cause I never want you to get ghost, and I am more worthy than most, so I would appreciate it if you didn't address me too your friends as your nigga,

because niggas are the compilers of ignorance, men are the compilers of persistence, and I persistently want to run into your heart with no head start, so therefore I can endure the competition that jumps the gun and fail to realize that winning the race of a woman has a lot more to do than with the speed you run, and hold off on the intercourse, cause yet that is a course that I see us sharing in the future,

I want us to enter into that course together after the playing field has been evaluated as being equally balanced out, see Sharee, you came to me lookin to be rebuilt, but I must break you down more, break down the wall cemented to your beating cardio frame, breakdown the stupid, dumb and worthless words embedded inside your brain, I must break down my own desires, to see your desire of once again being happy become complete, and that Ms. Sharee, is what I call, a perfect construction *project, because no jet will ever 9/11 this. P.S. I want you to be the man to read this to me and reconstruct me*

Yeah, this woman was crazy. She wrote a poem as if a man wrote it to her in hopes that another man would read this to her and build her back up from whatever she had went through. From this, I could tell that she hadn't been hurt by any man. I realized all men who dealt with her were smart and got the hell out of dodge when they finally realized how crazy she was. I let out a sigh, folded the letter back up in the box and crashed out until the morning.

That next afternoon, I went to the police station and told my story. Luckily, Detective Ahmad Parks was on duty. He was a regular at a lot of venues I frequented, and we kept a good, mutual relationship whenever we seen each other. He told me he would go check the cameras and see if they could get a positive ID. Even better, one of the forensics guys stayed in the same neighborhood I did, so he would have him keep an eye out. It was good to have friends in high places.

The next day, I called the security company who had installed the alarm system in my house and had them install two cameras. One would be placed at the front entrance of my house and the other in the backyard area. This way, I could monitor any and everyone who came out of my crib. I still felt tense, but I was a little bit more at ease. I called Mark to tell him about the story. In one sense he thought it was funny. In another sense, he knew how scary this was. He also called up some friends in law enforcement to be extra alert. Thank God for good people.

A few days went by with no disturbances. No knocks at the door. No crazy woman jumping out of the toilet when I took a piss at Benihana's. None of that went down. I was gravy. I visited Mr. Johnson in his downtown office just to chit chat and pass some time by. He was still my go to guy when it came to publishing. He knew a lot of what I had been through, so he wasn't in a rush to get me back to shooting out 4 or 5 projects a year. Heck, why would he worry? He had quite a few prosperous clients.

I wrapped that up and headed back home. As I turned up the street, I noticed something different. Everyone's trash can was still on the sidewalk. My trash can, however, was gone. I immediately reversed it around the corner, not thinking that I may run into somebody's car. I parked the car, called Parks and told him what was going on. I knew I had a crazy woman stalking me, but there was now a chance that she was now messing with my property. About 20 minutes later, he arrived with another squad car behind him. We talked about how this was going to work.

First, he made a call to the security company to see if any alarms had went off, and to check the feed from the video cameras. They reported back a negative on both, so I was a little bit more at ease. We then headed to my house. The plan was for me to go inside of the house with two officers as trailers. I didn't think much of anything was about to occur, seeing that no alarms were picked up. Hey, maybe one of my neighbors read my book and put my trash bin back by the gate. I was thinking all kind of crazy scenarios. Oh well. I opened the door with Adams and another officer behind me, turned the corner and I got the shock of my life.

***

"Miss let em see your hands!!!," Ahmad barked out. This crazy woman was sitting at my dining room table, crying her eyes out so hard that her mascara had run down her face.

"So that's it?," she said in a whimpering voice. "You didn't like your gift?? You don't love me?"

"Ma'am, bring your hands up from under the table. Put them where I can see them." Ahmad barked out one more time. As he walked up to her slowly, all of a sudden there was a *POP!!!* This crazy bitch had a gun and shot Ahmad. With a rage look in her eyes she pointed the gun at me. As I ran for a back room, I heard another *POP!* and I fell.

I heard footsteps. If I had been shot, the feeling didn't kick in yet. I thought this was it. She was coming to finish the job. I thought about my mom and everyone else whom I would never see again. Just then, I heard someone shout

"Stay with me Ahmad!!!" It was the other officer. I turned around to see Ahmad clutching his stomach and gasping for breath.

"I'm okay. Just get me a damn ambulance," he said with a very muffled voice. I immediately got up and ran to his aid. His back up from down the street came flying in after the call, and an ambulance was on their way. His partner had shot that crazy bitch. In about ten minutes, they arrived. This small, quiet neighborhood was now rocked with murder. It was sad enough that two people lay in my house bloody, one fighting for life and one dead.

Now, my neighbors were probably gonna look and treat me very different. Hell, I hadn't seen any color over here besides me in the two years I was here. Right now though, that was the least of my worries. Police and news crews soon swarmed the area. Here we go again. I was already plastered over the news once for being shot. Now, I would be plastered for a murder happening at my house. As they drove Ahmad off to the hospital, all I could think in my head was *what the hell will happen next???* Shit couldn't get any worse.

CHAPTER 15

All these negative incidents had finally taken its toll on me. My girl died, my baby died, crazy bitches in my house, I got shot and even the city hopping and partying was draining me. Luckily, Ahmad survived his bullet wound, so at least another body wouldn't be under my belt.It's a hell of a lot more things that have happened over these last few years that I just choose to keep to myself. I was tired of what I was doing.

I was starting to lose my passion for writing. If all this is what comes along with being successful, I really didn't want it. I had everything I wanted, but I wasn't happy anymore. It was time for me to leave for a long time and lose contact with everyone.

A week after the incident, I took care of all my personal stuff for the next two months. Being a multi millionaire had its advantages, as I could afford that luxury. I called Mark, but he didn't answer. I left him a voicemail and told him I was going away for a while. I didn't tell him where, because I didn't want anyone to know. I packed up about a month worth of clothes. I really didn't know where I was going to go. I sat on my living room couch and just zoned out. Someone was calling me, but I could give two damns about that now. All I remember was bursting into tears, head cocked back and looking up at the ceiling. Why was I not happy when I had everything I had ever wanted in life?

I know some people automatically think that I need Jesus. However, I went to church when my schedule permitted it. I had a fondness of God. Sure, I wasn't a saint, but I did give him all the glory for what he blessed me with. This had nothing to do with him. This had everything to do with me. Finally, after what seemed like hours of crying, I picked up the phone and called the airport. I asked about any flights headed to Australia. They informed me that there was one leaving that night, and that there were some last minute cancellations.

I said screw it. I paid a little extra for a first class ticket, drove to the airport and got on that plane. I was going to have one high ass parking lot fee, but I really didn't care. It was time for me to find a new me. It was time to get the hell away from everyone and just enjoy life for a while. These 23 hours in the air would be the last little bit people seen of Terelle. The minute I would step foot off the plane, the new me would be reborn.

I arrived at the Perth Int'l airport after what seemed like forever. One thing I can say, if the females on the plane reflected what was going to be here, at least my eyes would be very well pleased. I was exhausted and just ready to hit my hotel room, but these bags were taking forever. Not to mention that this airport was the size of New York City. Maybe it was my jet lag, I really couldn't tell. All I know is that I got tired of walking quick.

Finally, my bags came. It was a good thing Australia has actual baggage boys, cause I for damn sure didn't feel like carrying anything. I first exchanged my money, which wasn't that much of a difference in Australia. They rolled my bags outside to a waiting cab, and I tipped them with a hundred, which was still pretty hefty in Aussie money after it got exchanged. My bags got loaded in, and I was off to my sanctuary for the next month: The Burswood Intercontinental Hotel and Casino.

I had purchased one of the most exquisite suites in that joint. $2,500 a night was surely worth it and no problem for me to pay at all. I figured hey, if I'm going to be M.I.A. for a month, I might as well be M.I.A. in style. Immediately after I checked in, my black ass went straight upstairs and went to sleep. I left at night, and it was mid afternoon over here, 1:30 to be exact. I set my alarm for 9 o'clock and crashed the hell out for some much needed rest. Dreamland the amusement park was going to get a full visit from me.

The alarm finally went off and it was time to enjoy this thing called vacation. I brushed my teeth, lathered up with the zest to get all 2,000 of my body parts, shaved and lined up the goatee to a crisp, and finally threw on a custom made mango suit, with the taupe lizard skins. I had plans on rolling high tonight, and the casino was the exact place for it. It was connected to the hotel, and I slid through ready to tear it down. I bypassed all the slot machines, poker machines or any other BS dollar game. This man right here was about to run wild on the craps table. I got ten thousand dollars worth of chips and went to work. I sensed everyone wondering who the hell I was. The Cartier frames hid my eyes, giving me a mystique to the fellow spectators.

I spent about an hour there, drinking for free and killing this damn table. I invested 10 G's worth and came out 45 G's richer. That's how they bred us in the Midwest. High risk, high reward. After cashing in, and avoiding every wanna be person who was trying to be my friend, I headed up to the club inside the joint called The Ruby Room. As I walked in, the voice in my head screamed **GOOD LAWD!!!!!!!!!**

Now, this is what you called a cool atmosphere. Everyone was dressed casual. Some on my level, others on a normal level, but you could look and tell that there wouldn't be any drama. I enjoyed the night and the great music. I danced, drank, danced, drank some more, danced and drunk even more. Around 3:15 in the morning, I was good and drunk, but still had sense enough to remember everything I was doing. Just then, there was a tap on my shoulder.

"Do you wanna dance?"

I turned around and seen the prettiest sight in my life. I had to focus because I know how liquor vision can mess things up for a brother, as they did in Vancouver some time back with two tons of fun.

"Yes beautiful. Let's do this." I grabbed her from the back as she slowly grinded those firm cheeks on a brother. Man, I hadn't felt this much closeness to a woman since my baby Karey died some time ago. I don't know why the DJ played R. Kelly feeling on your booty, but all I knew was that baby girl booty felt nice. Once the song ended, we conversed for a little bit. Her name was Tamera. She was light skinned, nice curly hair and stood about 5'8. She had a banging body and she was on vacation out here for three weeks teaching dance classes.

Ironically, she was also resided in San Diego, so this was something I chose to pursue. She was also staying in the same hotel as I. She was pretty tired at this point, so after our convo, she gave me her room number and told me to swing through around 2 tomorrow so we could get up for lunch. This amazed me. I was drunk, but she wasn't giving it up on the first meet and greet. This I liked. As for me, I kept the party going even after she left until about 5 in the morning. That's when I left, walked back to my hotel room and crashed out. If this first night was a symbol of what was to come for the next 29 days, this was going to be a trip to remember.

***

I went down to Tamera's room on the 8th floor around 1:30 to get this thing started. As she opened the door and greeted me with an adorable "Hi," I noticed the instant beauty. No make up, just pure gorgeousness. Damn, where the hell was she at in San Diego. We immediately struck up a conversation and headed down to catch a cab to head out. Enjoying the ride along the beautiful ocean, you would've thought we were two little kids. We laughed the whole time until we finally decided to stop at a serene restaurant along the ocean. Inside, we started detailing our past, as I learned she was a few years removed out of her own relationship that ended. As we grubbed and talked, the story about the club incident came up.

"Yea, so I hear the shots...and a brother started running." I thought I was doing nothing but making mere conversation. All of a sudden, the look on her face changed drastically.

"Excuse me," she said, as she proceeded to step in the courtyard area. I was stunned. Was it something I said? Did a brother have some shit on his face??? I calmly got up and followed her to the courtyard.

"Tamera?" I could obviously see that she was distraught. Her arms were folded and head buried crying tears. Just then, she began to talk.

"A few years ago, my boyfriend was at that same party. He was kind of on the wrong side of things. Long story short, his street life caught up with him that night. He was gunned down. Gunned down in cold blood!!!"

Just then, she keeled over at the waist as I grabbed her to console. I couldn't believe this. How random was it that our lives intertwined many moons ago on one faithful evening? The same night I got shot, her man lost his life. Life was indeed too damn short and the world was too damn small.

CHAPTER 16

I had a lump in my throat as I thought of how to respond to her. I was seeing myself in the hospital again with Karey crying above my bed. "Well,"as I paused for a quick moment to collect my thoughts. "I was there that night when your boyfriend got shot. I ended up getting shot in my leg fleeing the scene. It was one of the scariest nights of my life."

Tamera suddenly asked to be excused for a minute. She went outside on the back patio of the restaurant, and I gradually followed behind. As the tears flowed down her face, I held her in my arms to allow myself to be her crutch. I barely knew this woman, but we were instantly connected due to one incident that we both wish that we could forget. Slowly, she wrapped her arms around me as to say thank you for embracing her heart.

"Thank You," she finally whispered as she wiped her eyes.

"Lets go back in and continue our good time." We walked in hand and hand. I don't know if she realized it, but I did. Maybe it was just a time in the moment. Maybe it was something deeper. I really didn't know. What I did know is that this wasn't like anything I had ever experienced with any other woman before.

We finished our lunch and headed down by the ocean. We sat on a grassy hill and just talked as if we were best friends. I don't recall how long we talked. All I remember was when we had finished, it was dark and my watch read 10:57. We caught a cab back to our hotel. On the way, she fell asleep on my shoulder. In that moment, many thoughts went through my head. Was this the beginning of a new beginning? Was this only a one time thing? Was this woman going to end up being crazy like a few I had encountered in my day?

All of these things crossed my mind. When we got to the hotel, I escorted her to her room, gave her a hug and we went our separate ways. I slept that night with a comfort I hadn't felt in quite some time. Over the next three weeks, we hung out together every day after she finished her dance seminars. We toured the city, enjoyed drinks and dancing out on the town. Most of all, we enjoyed great conversation.

One morning, I invited her up to my room. We decided we would have just a chill day with movies and room service. She loved scary movies like me, and the Saw series was perfect. After we made it through breakfast, lunch, some snacks and the first five Saws, we just cut everything else and talked. We went through every event throughout our lives. I found out she was more like the female version of me. She was born and raised in SouthEast San Diego, brought up in the Skyline section. It wasn't East Chicago, but they had their fair share of violence, drugs and poverty. Like me, her father died at twelve, except he was killed on a drug deal gone wrong. Her mom lost custody of her two years later as she battled an alcohol addiction and repeat financial woes. She took on the rest of her adolescent years being raised by her grandmother and using dancing as an outlet to stay away from the perils of the streets.

It was truly enlightening to hear her story. Too know that I had someone in my life who could relate to my upbringing was quite refreshing. I had gotten her number before she left, and we agreed to continue this once I returned. I was glad that she didn't think we were dating. You know how some people think because you go out a few times that you are dating that person. Those are the people who have messed up the whole dating scene by trying to make their own rules up. I blame emotional ass dudes for this, because they in turn influence the females who really didn't know any better. I was so glad to be from the Midwest, because we knew the game. We had pimp wisdom and hoe knowledge by the time we were three.

I enjoyed my last nine days in Perth, and headed back to San Diego on that long 23 hour flight. This time though, I had a one day layover in Hawaii, and I used it too my full advantage. I hit up Zanzibar's nightclub down in Waikiki. It was a cool hip hop spot, not to mention that those Navy boys were deep in there. I didn't even know these dudes, but they showed me mad love. These sons of bitches knew how to party, and I learned first hand

120

that the term drink like a sailor was factual. After a bomb night, I headed back to the airport hotel, got some sleep and woke up the next morning to fly back out to Los Angeles. The flight was a quick five hours, and my connection to San Diego was an hour later. Once I was back in the air, I was at ease, knowing that I would soon be back in my city, in my car and heading to the crib.

I touched down in San Diego at seven in the morning. I was rejuvenated and ready to see my bed for the first time in God knew how long. I finally cut my phone back on. I didn't want to be bothered until I got back in the city. Man oh man, my phone buzzed so damn much with missed messages that I wanted to break that damn thing. I listened to every kind of message while waiting for my bags.

I had ones for business, personal, my mama cursing me out, my mama cursing me out again, Mark snapping off, business, personal and finally, my mama cursing me out once again. Thank God I didn't have to see her face to face. I got my bags and headed to my whip. I cranked my baby up, paid that outrageous $720.00 parking fee and dipped out to the freeway, heading to my place which I called the crackhouse.

I got to the house and didn't even pull my bags out of the car. I went in the crib, headed upstairs and just jumped on the bed. I let out one big AHHHH. Damn, it felt good. I felt rejuvenated and reborn. I had met a great woman and had a great time in a foreign country. Most of all, I got my mind right. I had a renewed passion for everything. Writing would never be the same for me. After what seemed like hours of rejoice, I finally got back into my norm. I pulled my bags out of the car, scooped up the bundles of mail and fixed me something to eat. Deep down I wanted a surf-n-turf burrito, but I hadn't been home in a month, so I owed it to myself to cook myself a home cooked meal. The spaghetti was boiling, the catfish was frying and I was living on cloud nine at the moment. I took time to sort through the mail, and I came across a strange piece of mail from Dallas, Texas. I thought it was an accident, but I could tell that it was handwritten and not typed out. I figured whoever wrote it had meant it for me. I opened it with no qualms, expecting nothing more than another person who was claiming to be my uncle brothers sister mamas cousin on my daddy side. You know how people come out of the woodworks as your family when you prosper and get rich.

As I read the letter, all of a sudden the food became irrelevant. What I was reading had to have been a joke. Just to make sure I wasn't hallucinating off some weed that I didn't know was in my system, I read the letter three more times. This Mr. John Wallace was claiming to be my real father. That wasn't what got me though. He was naming details about my life that only me and my mother knew. I finished up cooking and immediately made a call to my mother back in Chicago. She picked up the phone, cursing my black ass out for disappearing, but I immediately cut her off.

"Mom?!!! Who is this guy John Wallace who just wrote me with some garbage talking about he's my real father?!!! He's telling me things about us that only me, you and dad should know. What is going on mom?!!!" All of a sudden, there was an eerie silence. I knew then that I had struck a nerve and that I was about to receive some news that I really didn't want to hear.

"T.J.," in a somber voice, " He's right. That's your daddy baby."

My heart dropped, along with the glass of orange juice that was in my hand. What the hell did I just hear? This man writes me out of nowhere, claiming to be my father, and its true.

"I'm sorry I never told you baby. I didn't want you to find out."

I was deeply stung inside. I had just came back from a 30 day vacation to release my mind, and now I was being hit with some news that put me back in a surreal mindset.

"Mom, no, no. Please tell me that this is some joke?"

"I'm sorry T.J, its not."

I could not believe this. I told my mom to hold on, as I prepped myself to hear this story.

CHAPTER 17

It was November of 1983. My mom was a very young 25 years old. She had done well for herself. She was a communications graduate from the University of Michigan, and was working for an IT company out of Madison, Wisconsin.

That was one thing about my mom. She was never scared to venture outside of her comfort zone to get herself established. Working for about a year, she had wanted to start back up on the dating scene. College days were long gone, and this was the time and age where people started to think about the long term.

There was no more Oh my goodness he is fine attitude in her system. What she wanted was oh my goodness; does he have his own like me? Does he have good credit, no priors, steady income, and a solid foundation? Those were the things that mattered in the mid 20's to early 30's, because looks don't pay the bills. I don't care how fine anyone is. If you're still in the house with mama after a certain age and not establishing yourself, then it is a problem. Potential? Naw, we were all born with that. Any who, my mom continued on with the story. One night towards the middle of November, my mom decided to head out to a local jazz spot in downtown Madison. As she enjoyed her night with a few wine coolers, she was approached at her table by a very well dressed man named John Wallace. Like her, he was a college graduate and had his own.

What stood out most about him was that he was very well dressed from head to toe. Conversation sparked up and the two hit it off immediately. They danced the night away and enjoyed good laughs. Afterwards, they took a trip to a diner that stayed open 24/7. Over some good ole breakfast food, they conversed on the aspects of their lives, and how they had gotten to the points in their lives where they were currently at. As they winded down, my mom asked if she could come home with him and continue to converse.

She knew her intentions, but back then, I guess people had a mindset where they didn't just want to come out and say they wanted to cut. They arrived at his home, and it didn't take long for things to go down. It turned into more than a one night thing. They continued to hang out, have sex, hang out some more and have more sex. A month and a half after they initially met, my moms friend who usually visited her monthly didn't come knocking at her door. She told John and it was devastating news to both of them. Neither didn't want children at this point in their lives, but they agreed mutually to keep me and raise me. As she said John put it, "It's not this baby's fault that they will be here. The least we can do is give it a chance at life, even if it would affect theirs." Nine months later, I was born as Terelle T.J. Wallace.

Over the first six months, things were great, as they both took part in my upbringing and made sure I had the best chance possible at life. Then, in March of 1985, things all of a sudden took a drastic turn. John's company had given him a promotion, but he had to move to Dallas and work in the big firm. This was a heartbreaker for my mom, as now she would have to become a single mother.

They discussed the parameters of the situation and came to a mutual agreement. He would send $1000 a month in support, and take me in the summertime, and alternate holidays when I got older. Until then, he would fly up once a month for when he had to return to Wisconsin for his monthly financial meetings with his company. That would at least give him a week with me. Things went well for quite some time, and all of a sudden, when I became two, things all of a sudden stopped. The money stopped, the visits stopped and the communication came to a halt.

My mom did everything in her power to get in contact with him, even calling his firm, but it was to no avail. They would not shell out any information, as they had no record of him having children in his file. This devastated my mother, and over the next two years, she had to put in what seemed like triple time just to see me have a chance. Financially, there was no problem at all.

She had a great career, but it was the aspect that I would no longer have a man in my life. As they say, only a man can teach a boy how to become a man. Around the age of four, my mom ran into the guy who would later become her husband, Mr. Samuel Washington. Over time, I remember him being the only male face I would see on a consistent basis, so to me, he was my dad. Two years later, him and my mother married, and we moved down to Highland Park, Illinois where he was an advisor at some big time firm that dealt with a lot of high profile athletes.

My mom had enough trust in him to follow his lead. She even changed my last name to his. He had grew up on the South side of Chicago, and always made it a priority to go back and help the community. We stayed there all the way until his death when I was twelve. To not keep me distant from his side of the family, mom gave up the suburb lifestyle and moved us down to East Chi. It wasn't a bad neighborhood we lived in, but it was far from the suburbs. Plus, even though we lived in an upper middle class neighborhood, we weren't to far from the hood. I didn't get the move at first, but later in life, I truly appreciated it.

I was closer to my uncles (my dad had five brothers) and they all took a hand in making sure that I would not fall to the perils of Chi streets. At the same time, they also took the time to show me the other side of what I had not seen, so that I may understand it and not be fearful if I was ever to come across it. To them, I owed a lot.

My mom was in tears by the end of the conversation as she felt bad for hiding the information from me for all these years. I told her everything was good and that it was no biggie. I couldn't be mad at this woman; after all she had done for me, especially after my father died. I told her to take it easy and come out here to visit. Reluctantly, as my mom always was when it came to doing something for herself, she finally agreed. I was ecstatic. I could bond with my mom and at the same time, spoil her. That was something she rarely did in her life, even though she was very successful. We talked for about another 30 minutes after she told me the story. Two days later, I purchased her a first class plane ticket to San Diego and it was on.

***

My mom arrived on schedule a week later and soaked in the sunny California air. My goodness, now I knew what she was feeling when I was a child. She wanted to go everywhere. I must've done a cross country trip in my car with this woman. Hey, she deserved it though. The malls, the restaurants, the spa treatment, everything she got, I had no qualms about giving her. Heck, we only have one mother in this world. It is our jobs as children to show them the love they gave us when we were children.

It was even more crucial for me, seeing that she played the role of mother and father. I even got the chance to introduce her to Tamera. I told her my mom was coming into town and T volunteered to cook dinner for her. It was a nice little meet up as all three of us chit chatted about life. Of course, my mom eventually got to ask her motherly questions, but we playfully brushed that notion off. She could see that we did like each other, but moms didn't go dwelling to deep. She respected my privacy enough to know when to pump the brakes. However, I knew the one on one questions were coming. As we headed back to the house on full stomachs, she started up the convo. "T.Jaaaaayyyyyy??"

Damn, I knew what this was already going to be about. "Yes mom," I said with a chuckle. She just looked at me with a little grin on her face.

"Ok mom. I like her. I like her a lot. This girl makes me feel good. Yes, I am going to pursue this relationship with her. Yes, I am going to try and make it work. Yes, I am glad that you approve of her."

My mom burst out laughing. Then, she told me something that re-ignited my spirit.

"Baby, mama always trusted you. Did you forget that I trusted your decision to forgo college to come out here and achieve your dream of becoming a writer?"

I paused for a minute and really marinated on what she said. She did in fact trust me with my decision. She never questioned it. She never down shot it or anything like that. She let me be a man, and allowed me to make my own way and learn from my own mistakes. I know we all love our mothers, but her reminding me of that made my love run even deeper for her. I love my mom!!!

CHAPTER 18

My mom had finally flown back to Chicago, but it wasn't to stay. Upon her last day here, I asked her would she feel comfortable being in a new surrounding. To my surprise, she agreed. Her intentions were to go back and sell the house, make a profit and come out here to enjoy the good life with her son.

I started the process of getting her a house built. Unlike other authors, I cranked out four or five classic novels a year. I feel that you have to stay in peoples faces for them never to forget who you are. I didn't want to be a one hit wonder. I wanted to be the person that people would wonder when my next big smash was coming out. That mentality had my net worth at almost twenty million dollars now. In about two months, mom sold the house for 200,000 more than what she had purchased it for. She donated all of the furniture to good will, sent her clothes off to my place and it was the beginning of a new life for her. She would no longer have to work for anything else in her life. All she had to do was sit back and reap the benefits of being a world class mother. Once she arrived, I took her to see what would soon become hers, and that was a beautiful three bedroom house with a huge backyard where she could have her own garden. Her eyes watered upon seeing where she would lay her head down for the rest of her life. She couldn't believe it.

"Mom, this is just my way of saying thank you." She couldn't even respond, as she continued to let the tears flow. I knew she was grateful to receive such a gift, but I was even more grateful to give it to her.

***

It was now late 2007, and things had remained consistent. My mom was loving life in her home. Me and Tamera had now been official for almost two years now. The speaking assignments continued, I put out a few more books and life was on the up and up. I myself moved out of my condo and across the street from my mother in a home I had purchased. I figured that we might as well be neighbors.

After long trips on the road where she couldn't see me, she wouldn't have to drive 3 miles down to my house. I could just walk across the street, talk to her and relax to a home cooked meal in which she always provided. Over at her house during a random cooking session, I had a deep conversation with her.

"Mom, I'm thinking about asking Tamera to marry me."

The stirring of the Pinto Beans and ham hocks came to a

complete stop as she gave me this stare. The only time I seen stares like this is when I had did something I had no business doing as a child. I was nervous as hell.

"So what are you asking me for? Man up, make her your wife and call it a day." I looked at my mama kind of crazy.

"So ma, you aint got nothing to say on this." She then put the spoon down on the counter and gave me her two cents.

"Look. You've been making grown man decisions since you were eighteen. I love her, but it don't matter what I think, nor what anyone else thinks. If you ready to marry her, then put the ring on her finger. Now, if you want advice on how to do the damn thing, then that's what mama is for. But mama isn't for approval. That stopped when you moved out and became you own man."

Damn, this woman had set me straight once again like she always did.

"Aight mom, what is the best way to propose to her?"

"One knee and catch her off guard. I'll leave it at that."

Now, I was thinking random shit in my head on what to do. Tamera was up in Sacramento teaching a dance class for the next few days. Wouldn't it be nice if I was to go up there and propose to her I thought? I told my mom about the idea, and all she had to say on it was

"Do it babe. Just make sure I'm with you when you buy the ring, because I know you men don't know jewelry like a woman."

Yea, she damn sure wasn't lying. The next day, we went ring shopping. Upon hitting the first store, I knew I had found it. It was a beautiful solitaire diamond.

"Mom, what about this? She would love this."

My mom took one look at it and said "Yea, she'd love it, if you were a normal guy."

Moms explained to me that some things are meant to splurge on. We as a people invest highly in our homes, clothes, cars and other things that matter to us. However, when it comes to investing for other people who deserve it, we sometimes slack. That was per the case of our government, as we seen they don't invest nothing into their own people, but they can damn sure invest millions upon millions of dollars studying the mating habits of frogs in the jungle. She was right though. We kept searching, and all of a sudden, my mom screamed.

"THIS IS IT!!!" They were red 1 carat diamonds meshed in white gold, topped off with a 1 ½ carat stone up top. The price, $6,000. I knew Tamera's ring size from all the rings she loved to wear, so I said screw it and copped it. My mom was ecstatic. The whole way back home she acted like a kid on Christmas saying

"I'm bout to be a grandma." She repeated that over and over a billion times. All I could do was laugh. She was looking far ahead, but that was the plan. I always wanted me three or four shorties. With Tamera, I knew that wouldn't be a problem, because she has some of that good stuff that a man did not want to come out of. Anytime the coochie makes that sound like you stirring up some macaroni and cheese, you know you got you one.

***

I called Tamera and told her I was flying up to Sacramento to spend time with her. Her classes for the last two days had been cancelled, so she was just relaxing in her hotel room and taking it easy. She was happy about this. She could spend her last two days up North with her baby. The date was November 24th and my flight was due to arrive at 6 p.m. sharp. It was only an hour and some change flight time, but I was the most nervous person on Earth at that time.

This was it. I was really about to ask a woman to marry me and become my wife. Ahh damn. Now I know what a prisoner feels like before they pull the switch on him. My southwest flight finally landed at the airport in Sacramento, and my baby was there to greet me. We embraced in a deep hug, kiss and talked as we waited for my bags to come around this carousel.

I really thought about dropping down right now and proposing to her at baggage claim, but hell naw. I knew she loved me, but I didn't want to take the risk of being turned down in front of a whole bunch of people. We got my stuff and headed fifty minutes East to Fairfield, Ca, where she was staying out of. Her last classes were supposed to be there, but now she was just sitting in a Bay Area city doing nothing. The whole time she was driving, I was slowly patting my pocket, making sure the box didn't fall out.

I had been doing this for the last few hours, because the last thing I wanted to do was reach in that pocket and not anything be there. We got to the hotel around 7:15 p.m. and settled in. After what seem like hours upon hours of talking, cuddling and watching TV, the clock finally struck 7:42. I went to the bathroom. It wasn't to piss, but rather to get my head right for what I was about to do. I came back out as she was sitting on the edge of the bed, clad in a mango sweater and tight fitting blue jeans.

"Tamera, you know I love you right?"

"Yes," she responded.

"You know I want to spend the rest of my life with you right?" With her eyes getting watery she again said yes. I then dropped down to one knee and pulled the box out of my pocket. I opened it up slowly.

"Tamera, will you marry me?" As she shook her head up and down, she let out a silent "Yes."

I slid the ring on her finger. In that quick moment, I thought about all the women I dealt with in my past. All those near misses and failures had led me to find the woman of my dreams. I couldn't believe that I was at this point in my life. As men, we are kind of bred to be these player and pimp type individuals. We aren't supposed to have emotions. However, I feel that there is nothing better than when a King meets his Queen.

I had indeed met my queen. We hugged, kissed and eventually emotions took over and we had us quite a few love making sessions. This was not just love making anymore with my girlfriend. She was now my fiancée and soon to be wife. It took on a whole new meaning. I was finally here, and feeling complete. I had a great career, with a great woman, with whom I would soon be married too. There were no complaints.

CHAPTER 19

We returned to San Diego and had a huge celebration with her family and friends downtown. I treated them all to a bomb Brazilian steakhouse called Rio de Gado. We kicked back, enjoyed laughs and bonded as a family.

Jackie and her fam were there as well. They were family to me. Even though the same blood didn't run through our veins, it didn't stop us from becoming fam. What amazed me more is that

Darrell's mom decided to bring this boy along. I knew he could eat, but damn!!! He just was inhaling meat. This boy really had a bottomless pit stomach. What made it even funnier is that in between him eating enough for mankind, he managed to blurt out of nowhere; "I like your girlfriend Uncle Mac."

All we could all do was laugh. That boy was certainly

something special. After my credit card got ran up higher than Giraffe cooch, everyone left except me and Tamera. We decided to continue our night doing our own thing. That thing was taking a long drive, enjoying the San Diego scenery and being big kids. We went from Coronado, all the way back up through La Jolla, and even took it further north to Carlsbad. This wasn't wasted gas to me. This was a chance for me to spend time with the one I loved the most. In my eyes, that was worth any amount of money I had to spend on gas.

Over the next few weeks, a lot of things changed. Tamera finally moved in with me. I had been wanted this to happen, but she insisted we stay in our own separate places until a moment like our engagement occurred, where we were sure we were going to be together for a long time. Maybe I should have waited a little longer; because I found out first hand what all men said was true. Women really do take over everything when they come in. I had to go and buy all new artwork because the walls were too bare for her.

My closet space was dramatically reduced, even though there were two unoccupied rooms with two unoccupied closets. What upset me the most is that my man cave disappeared. It became her study room. You can do whatever you want, but you never mess with a man's man cave. However, the term happy wife, happy life is said for a reason. If a woman isn't complaining, then you are definitely living the good life. This was definitely fun for me. I was slowly preparing to become a husband, and I was learning the rules slowly but surely.

I now concentrated on my next book project and also my

poetry. I took the pen one night after washing and detailing my baby's car to write her a poem I entitled Drippin:

Buttnaked...drippinwet...glistenin..glistenin...glistenin, water flowin' from the lips of your cliffs that I look to climb and explore from top to bottom, and as the sun comes out and dries everything up, I open my mouth up and catch every drop that drips for the saturation of my organs, cause its a fact, we need liquid to live, and I choose to sip a different form of H2O, matter fact, its more refreshing, so much more that I even choose to take a dive in it on a regular basis, and like meat in the oven, that liquid stays bastin' my meat to ensure it stays tender during the cookin' process, drippin' with juices, that how you know ya meal has been cooked right, and bump what they say, there is nothin' like a late night meal to quell the hunger of the stomach or my life stick,

drip, drip, drip, the same sound made as when that leaky pipe connects with the bucket using to catch the fluid, I become the repairman, purposely messin' up to cause an overflow and put this system out of commission for longer than expected, this maintenance will take a while to complete, drip...drip...drippin', its like drug flippin', I inject you with this hypodermic and its fills your void, head swaying on the inside from the ride this dose is given' you, foaming at the mouth, releasing liquid from a different place cause you couldn't stand the needle just being stuck in, you had to get a direct taste, and you savored it all, catchin' every drop of this sexual heroin, drip...drip..drippin' no more, now its like you are a complete waterfall, damn that, like a raging river who broke through the dams that were meant to contain it,

now aint it amazing that your walls have been broken down, no more thinkin' about what used to be, its all about what is occurring now, cause now, you enjoy the rush, lust never felt so damn good, messed you up so much you started confusin' hoods, cause he bust you open so good that when you came, you were throwin' up pitchforks while yellin' on the five, he messed you up big time, but in a good way,

had you drippin' down streets and soakin' through sheets, causin' Mr. plumber man to work extra hours on the job, cause now the job had been done, the rush of this love mixed with lust had you bustin,' over and over again, and now, your whole house was flooded, from all the unrepaired drips, so excuse me miss, let me help clean up, by takin' another sip

I was so geeked, that I messed around and wrote her two more. They were entitled "Real Lovers" and "Satisfaction"

Real Lovers:

Pull back the door and watch me work before I even begin to touch, see eyeballs locking creates lust before it starts, what's about to go down is deeper than any thought that was processed, because thoughts can't amount to the efforts put forth in action, satisfaction is the key, courtesy of teases, bite marks and fingernail scratches, two souls latch on to one another, exchanging spiritual connections that are invisible to the naked eye, love so good that souls die and spirits come alive, cause to make love and touch the others spirit, that's when you'll hear it, the moans, the screams, the deep breaths, physical touch can only offer up a mere sampling of this, but yet it still aint got nothin' on this, that spiritual connect, wet has never felt so good, and someone being a hard head is actually appreciated for a change, breaking down this multi million dollar love into change as positions change, front, back, and side to side like T.I.P, while Teddy P. plays in the background, from the ground back up to the bed sheets,

their soaked with love juice as the thoughts of them both think of tasting each others juice, he will have remnants upon his face, she on the other hand will savor the full taste, not wasting a drop as she wipes off the lil mess that dribbles down her chin, and with a grin, she gladly says thank you and he responds you welcome, see in this love, there is no fear of doing it all, because they give each other their all and they both realize, what they wont do, someone else will, and the second purpose of their thrill is that they don't want each other thinking about that past fling,

cause the worst is to get fucked while your lover is thinking of someone else, that's why I say if you scared go to church, or boast yourself up, cause the worse thing ever is to love someone forever, and not do what needs to be done, cause you don't wanna be that woman or man whose mate runs back to the one who satisfied all of their sexual needs whether physically or mentally, and real lovers know this.

Satisfaction:

Studies have shown that the mouth is the dirtiest part of the human body, while the hidden gems of the same body are the cleanest...and like the old timers used to preach that they'll wash your dirty mouth out with soap, I could only hope that two people in love wash theirs out with each other's sacred gems, but going out on a limb, some have this hidden fear of oral delight, minds stuck in a high school limelight or thoughts of not doing right is the wrong way to be, see when you in love with that lady, its your job as a man to kiss all of her lips, sift your tongue through her hips motions and taste her clear lotion that coats your cavities...ladies, when you in love with that man, its your job to do all you can to baste his stick,

lots of spits, moans and groans...cause good dome will remind him of why he keeps this house a home, his medication that you work out of the syringe makes him cringe, and you ingest with pure delight...but nowadays...for some reason...this ain't right, excuse after excuse is made, and beds become left unmade, one wants the other to do for them while they don't wanna return the favor,

its like they sayin its a crime to savor the flavor of your partner and I just don't get it, he says she bleeds so its not ethical, she says its the feel of it that makes her avoid it all, he says its too mushy on his face, she said she had a horrible experience blowin another man, I say they have that toilet bowl love cause they both full of shhhhhhhh...now I truly know the reason for side men and side chicks, cause those who don't wanna do the ones they love to the fullest extent, they leave the door open for these others to put in their applications, and relationships are now hiring part time stimulation, all because people are scared to do what their job requires.

Oh yea, the kid was back and back with a vengeance.

CHAPTER 20

It had been two weeks since my babe accepted my proposal. I figured I would finish up one more book project entitled "Second Time Around." It would be a simple novel about a couple who broke up and came back together a few years later to live happily ever after. It would be complex, yet something simple.

I kept it that way because I was more concentrated on getting our wedding day plans put together. We were going to have our ceremony on Valentines Day of 2009. To me, that would be the best New Year's gift I could ever receive, which was marrying my love on the day of love. I had the finance to make it a blowout wedding, but we were both still simple, so we went a different route. We were going to get married in a huge outdoor ceremony in Coronado. After that, we would head to a rented out mansion in Del Mar with some catered soul food and drank. We didn't want all that typical cake, pie and salad BS. WE BLACK!!!! We wanted some good ol collard greens, hot water cornbread, deep fried catfish, spaghetti, baked Mac-n-cheese, chitlins with hog maws, potato salad, black eyed peas with some juicy ass ham hocks, shrimp-n-grits, salt pork and to top it off, kool-aid in the red flavor!!!!!! See what a lot of people don't understand is that this is our culture.

Food brings us together, and for a monumental event like this, we wanted that food that touched people's soul. This wasn't gone be like the movie Soul Food where somebody was dying. This was going to be a party full of food and booze. I hit up one of my cousins back in Chi to cross the border over to Indiana and hit up his connect. I know Indiana had that official corn whiskey, a.k.a. moonshine. My West Coast peeps wouldn't be ready for that. Also, I started to get the drink list together. Cognac, Hennessey, Jack Daniels, Goose, Patron, Four loko, Crown and all that other good shit that destroyed our livers.

This right here would be the mother of all weddings. As the weeks continued to pass, I grew more and more nervous. I finished my novel, but my team advised me not to release it. I knew deep down it wasn't my best work, and they for damn sure seen that it wasn't. Talking to Mark, he informed me to just concentrate on the wedding. He reminded me that I was good. I dropped a minimum of four books per year, and they all sold well. It would be okay to take a break. Plus, having the benefit of earning income through speaking also would help me relax. Time ticked down and ticked down and ticked down even more.

New years passed, my mom grew another year older and it was now February 7. There could only be one thing to happen on this night. THE BACHELOR PARTY!!!!!

***

Me and Tamera had agreed to not see each other the whole week leading up to the wedding. I had one week until she took my last name forever. Tonight, I was just hoping that I didn't forget that I had a fiancé.

"MUTHAFUCKA LETS GET IT CRACKIN!!!!" That was Mark for ya. He was more crunk than me as we were driving down the highway to his pad in Mira Mesa. I knew how he and women were, so I was only imagining what this party was going to be like. We finally pulled up to the house, and I took a deep breath. Here we go.

"WHATS GOOD YOU OL SELLIN YA SOUL ASS NIGGA???!!!!!!!!!" That was my partner Deuce in there, already drunk and it wasn't even 9 p.m. My dude Slim was also in the building chillin, and watching the NBA game. This was our bond time, as we laid out the food trays of sandwiches and wings. That's all any brother needed at a bachelor party and we was cool.

For the next two hours as my boys filed in, we just chopped it up on some G-stuff, reflecting on good times and bad times. Then, 11:30 hit. Six bad ones walked in, along with there personal security and headed to the back. Aah damn, it was about to go down. The brothers started shaking me, making sure I was ready to go out on a high note. Man, I wasn't gone cheat on my lady, but you could best believe I would have me a handful of ass and breasts. The lights got dim, Ludacris P-Poppin got put on and the first stripper came out.

"Which nigga is the groom?" Everyone pointed to me as I sat on the couch, trying to remain calm looking at this thicker than grits woman.

"Aight, well if yo name aint groom, move the fuck off the couch."

My niggas scattered, as she climbed on top of a nigga and started grinding. All I seen was a pair of oiled up titties, until the second girl came around and did her thing. I was damn near delusional. Next thing I remember was being ass naked, laying on the floor with hot ass candle wax on my chest and some naked hoes doing some freaky things to me. I was feeling dollar bills hit me, and hearing nothing but commotion.

I also heard the sounds of a bitch getting rammed. I didn't know by whom, but she was damn sure getting it as I heard the screams. This party went on until about four in the morning, and I was indeed satisfied. Once the smoke cleared and the lights came on, all we did was share laughs and review the video that this nigga Mark recorded. I'll be damned!! I could not believe what I saw. I know damn well this video better not ever get out.

There was dicks getting sucked, pussy getting licked, candle wax, fire and one nigga I aint even know chillin in the corner eating wings and beating his damn meat at the same time. Hot damn!!! I didn't even think about what my baby's bachelorette party was like. I know she probably had a few dicks swinging in her face. Oh well, if she did, I couldn't be mad at her. All I knew is that in one week, she would be my wife. That day came a lot faster than I thought. It was now February 14th, and I was in the stretch Hummer limo trying to get my thoughts together. I told me boys to leave me alone as I thought about my journey to this point in my life. In 30 minutes, the beginning to the rest of my life would occur. The last thought I had before I got out of the car was of Karey. She was supposed to be here. I loved Tamera too death, but I could never forget what that woman meant to me. With a last I love you; I stepped out the limo and prepared to do the damn thing.

Everyone was now seated. I quickly scanned the rows of people as I waited on the altar. I whispered and I love you to my mom as she wiped her eyes. Everyone was smiling and chipper. I really couldn't comprehend what was about to happen until Jodeci's "Love U 4 Life" cut on. Everyone stood as Tamera was escorted out by her favorite Uncle. I know it was hard not having a father to escort her down. We were in the same boat. My pops wasn't there either. However, I just knew I was about to be a married man. We joined hands as she arrived at the altar. The look in each others eyes was priceless. Rev read her vows, but I had written my own. I did my poetry thing with them too:

THIS RING:

See this ring isn't just a material thing, this is more than diamonds inside of precious metal, this is God sealing symbolism that the devil can't even interfere with, cause with this, love is expressed til the death, and even in that, we will meet in the

Heavens, but for this time on Earth, it is like the birth of a new child, the new beginning for two souls, spirits and hearts interlocked with no key that can unlock this safe in which our hearts are protected, this ring, symbolizes the life journey that shall be walked, not ran, cause marriage is not a race, it is a slow marathon that shall be paced at a snail's pace,

that way, each moment in time can go by slow, and can be enjoyed to the max, so take this ring, place it on a finger not for decoration, but for declaration, to declare the love of two souls, Me and You, as we share the gift of giving each other to thee, and letting no influence of outside deceivers ever break this bond, this connection, see this is more than affection, this is looking into each others eyes to realize what really lies ahead, and what lies ahead is simple, the journey of a lifetime.

Everyone in the audience dropped tears along with my wife. I can see the look in her eyes not only told me it touched her heart, but it turned her on as well. I could tell that the honeymoon would be wild. Rev asked us, we both said I do and sealed it with a kiss. This was it. She was now officially Tamera Washington, and I was officially off the market. We went to the mansion that night and celebrated with family and friends. We tore the backyard up. Everybody was full, and half the people were drunk. It was alright, because we had 12 bedrooms in here so there was enough room for the drunks to lay their heads. This was indeed the best day of my life.

CHAPTER 21

"Man Granddad that was one helluva journey. I never knew so much had happened when you were young. I'm glad to have you as my grandfather. I love you." I then hugged my grandson Terrelle Washington III.

We were the only ones remaining in my home. Everyone else had left. My day was shot, but my grandson really lifted my spirits. As he headed upstairs to go to bed, I sat in my recliner and looked at my family picture.

Myself, Tamera, our two boys and my princess. It seemed like yesterday we were young and running wild. Now, I would have to live the remainder of my days without my backbone. Seeing her laid to rest today destroyed me inside. 52 years of marriage was a very long time. Everything in this house reminded me of her from the picture of my deceased mother who treated her as if she was her own, to the kitchen countertop where my second son Edward was conceived. People take love for granted nowadays. I learned from watching others when I was younger. My great grandparents were married for 72 and a 1/2 years before my great grandmother passed, leaving my gramps alone until it was his time to pass on. That's what I lingered for when I became married. I see these kids nowadays, and everything is 5 minutes instead of 5 years.

At the first sign of trouble, they bail. It happened back in my day as well, but now eternal love seemed extinct. I slowly cried off and on as I rocked back and forth. We had always watched TV together and she would cuddle up with me on the recliner. She knew it got on my damn nerves, because there wasn't a lot of room on that thing. However, she was my baby and that was all that mattered. How was I going to comprehend life without my love? That was my biggest question.

I drove back to the cemetery the next day to look at my baby's grave and talk to her one on one. I still had the same passion I had for her that I had the first time that I told her that I was deeply in love with her. I just stared at her marble clad grave, with fresh flowers, bears and balloons left by lots of people. Me however, I kept it simple and just dropped my baby a poem in an envelope. I also recited it to her.

A KISS

Kiss me like there's no tomorrow in your future,

like the next three seconds will be the last breaths you take on this Earth, kiss me as if you wanted me to inhale your past out of your system and into mine so I could digest it and crap it out, because those men were full of shit anyway, kiss me and talk to me in tongues, kiss me and tell me the stories of your inner most desires just from the touch of your lips, see a kiss is more than what a lot of people think, its my way to communicate without telling' you a word, its my way to seal the love letter I write with penetration, its my way to shut you up when I feel you talking too much, and trust, a real woman don't mind being hushed for the right man, see in my honest opinion,

I think the kiss was created in God's essence, cause He kissed the Earth upon creation, He kissed it goodbye with the flood, He blew a kiss to us when He came back for the second time, and His last kiss going to be the kiss of death, and we all know those are fire, so when you kiss me girl, you aren't necessarily kissing God, you just kissing the man He chose to represent you, see a kiss got more meaning that what you'll ever think, when I plant my seed, I'll get on my knees and kiss the belly of the garden in which its planted in, and then kiss the tree that sprouts from that soil, and we'll repeat this *process, until you feel there's enough plants to satisfy your vision of Eden, see my kiss ain't just a kiss, its a symbol of solidification, my kiss gives you internal orgasms for you to release later, my kiss is our equal common denominator, my kiss is me transferring love to your lips, and last I checked*

I got two pairs to kiss cause I can't give attention to one without giving attention to the other, and those other lips get kissed in the dark under covers, see a kiss is not merely a kiss at all, not to me at least, its an attaching of two into one, yet only a fraction of how much love is truly shown between two lovers.

I cried as the words rolled off of my lips. I knew she heard me in the spiritual form. However, not being able to see her in the physical, smiling after I recited one of my works to her, drove me crazy. Poetry and dancing, our two gifts, that kept us connected. I showed her love through words. She showed me love thru movement. She taught me how to salsa, and all kinds of other crazy forms of dancing. Also, it came in handy in our intimate times. The night we made our little girl Terri, she came home to a candlelit room, roses and a poem on the bed entitled

"Scorpio Freak"

They tell all men that when we succeed in life to never forget where we come from, so maybe that's

why we love pussy so much, pussy that runs like a faucet, so no need to worry bout we toss it, see I got my own personal story bout my own personal freak, her real name was Monique, but I simply called her my Scorpio freak, under the sheets, she was more of a damn beast than a creature with six legs, but the two she had parted ways like the Red sea to expose those wetlands that were underneath, so like a tamed Leo beast, I took her to the circus, she called my tongue an acrobat the way it balanced and performed on her trapeze wire, the roar of the crowd inside aroused her desire even more for a top ten performance, enormous flips and balancing acts had her laying flat, exhausted as all to be damn, I thought I had her in the palm of my hand with a tight grip, but when her five fingers balled up into a fist, she started to punch back, it all started when she pushed me on my back and proceeded to continue this circus act, her first trick was to make a rabbit pop up out a hat, only to take that magic wand and make it disappear again, and trust, that rabbit was nowhere in sight,

she ensured he was camouflaged well in one of her burrows, and I moaned like a straight bitch, all I felt was hot saliva drippin down my magic stick but still, I thought I had this, that was until she stopped and jumped on top, I was now her Ferrari, and she was driving in stick shift, had me hittin my clutch so I didn't leak my cars fluids prematurely, but surely, she was gonna get me to that point where I would eventually blow a gasket and I would need a full body repair, I then picked her up and put her in the air, I thought I had this, but to this chick, this wasn't ish, she bit my bottom lip, and flipped her tongue toward my ear canal to whisper, Fuck me as if this would be the last time you could use your dick,

who say that ish, so I began to bang it out while the pussy stung back, see I forgot that stinger she had toward the back was powerful, it could paralyze a man with one sting, but she showed me mercy on this occasion, I had never been in this situation, dealing with a woman who could take it like a champ and make that thang bite back, so when we finished messing up the sack, I kept wondering why this woman was such a beast, then I remembered, her birthday was November 19th, she was a Scorpio freak, and that's all that needs to be said about that

Once she read that, it was heaven. All I remember was me being sat down in a chair, a nice, slow wind being commenced by her and orgasms followed. That was quite possibly the greatest night of fucking we ever had. Notice people I said fucking, not lovemaking. After giving words to your woman like that, no slow sex was allowed.

***

Two years passed, and I was now 79. I saw my grandchildren surrounding me.

"Pull through Granddaddy."

That was my granddaughter Kilah, my daughter's oldest of five. I couldn't respond as I had a tube going down my throat. This old age had finally caught up with me. I didn't have cancer, or any other debilitating disease. I was just old, tired and ready to be with my wife for eternity. I motioned my hand as if I was writing. One of my babies handed me a pen and paper. I cracked a little smile and wrote,

"My time is now." I handed it back and all I could see was weeping. I heard nothing but cries of stay with us. I understood their pain, but I remembered that I had many poems sealed in envelopes that I never read to my wife. It was time for her to hear them. With one last glance, I smiled as big as I could, closed my eyes and my heart stopped. Hearing nothing else, I saw a light and went towards it. Tamera, Jesus, here I come.

ABOUT THE AUTHOR

Joe McClain, or better known as Joe Mac, is a seasoned spoken word artist who has taken his gift of writing to an extraordinary level. As an active duty military man, his travels around the globe have led to many cultural experiences, which influences his writing heavily. The young man from East Chicago, IN, who now resides in San Diego, hopes to be a huge influence to inner city youth to find their expression in literary forms instead of through the streets. Besides writing, he has shared the stage with several Def Jam poets and even took his talents to such places as Guam. His influence has been felt worldwide, but more work is to be done. One quote sums up the type of person he is: I learned to stop saying "I wish" and started saying "I will" a long time ago. Then, I learned to stop saying "I will," and I just did it. Then, once I did it, I did it some more. Through all of that, I learned the one thing to never say is "I can't."

ALSO AVAILABLE

"Freeze mother fucker!" a cop spat, but the Skyline hardhead wasn't trying to hear it. He blindly reached on the floor for his gun as he slowly regained his eyesight. Jail wasn't an option for the young rida. He knew he had done too much to turn back. Fuck it, he was gonna hold court in the streets. As he placed his hand on the gun that laid dormant on the floor, that would be as close as he got to picking it up and letting off a shot...

UPROCK PUBLICATIONS PRESENTS

LET ME PIMP
OR
LET ME DIE

=Till Game Do Us Part=

a novel by
CAUJUAN AKIM MAYO

As JP was hanging up the phone Yuki was walking down the track towards him. Perfect timing, JP thought to himself. He called Yuki over and introduced her to her new wife-in-law. "Yuki, this is your new wifey Kathy, also known as Green Eyes. Green Eyes, this is Yuki. Welcome to the family." The girls smiled and got acquainted. "How much you got on you?" JP asked Yuki.

"I made $400 more daddy."

"Alright good job, excellent work. That brings your total to $2,000. Since the nights been so good to us all, we're gonna take it in early and get to know each other better." JP had the best night of his life. Between the 2 hoes he took in $3,150, bumped a new hoe, and was now 2 deep with no sleep. Life was good, and it was only gonna get better.

UPROCK PUBLICATIONS PRESENTS

FAMILY HONOR

~The Seed~

Timmy O'Neil Charity

"That's enough!" Silence filled the room, as two muscle bound gorillas moved away from the two men hanging by their shackled wrists. Both men wore handcuffs, as a steel chain was looped over the beam in the ceiling. They were stripped to the wrist, exposing their battered and bruised torsos, which matched their equally distorted faces.

The men were best friends. Having grown up together in the reform schools of Virginia, they solidified their brotherhood as they furthered their education on the mean, brutal streets of Richmond, aka Richtown. Neither man was afraid to die, because they knew they had fucked up. But the man carrying out their punishment, had did more than wreck havoc on their bodies. They had committed treason. And that caused him to lose their trust in them. "This is how you treat friends?"

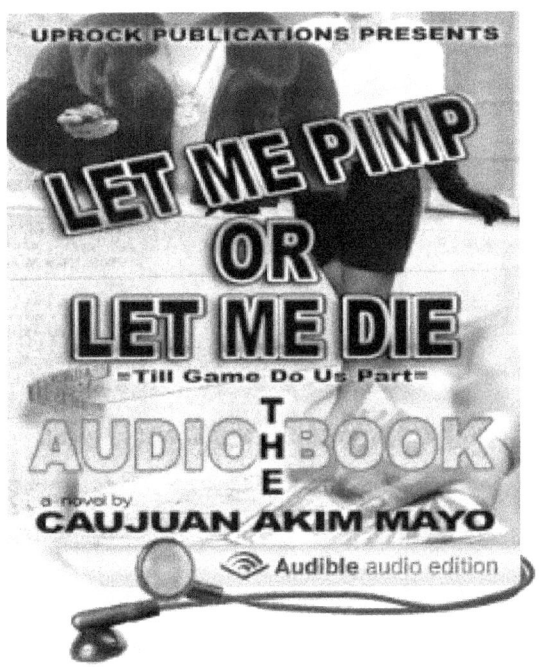

Don't have the time to read? Well, we have the solution. Pick up your audio version of "Let Me Pimp Or Let Me Die." The book by Caujuan Akim Mayo that started it all. Listen to this action pack audio book, loaded with special sound effects and cinematic music for dramatic effect, like no other audio book you've ever heard before. This is the audio book, that changed the game and set the bar.

Let Me Pimp Or Let Me Die 2, tells the story of a few female workers in the "Game," told through their lives as you see and find out what motivates a woman to start ho'n and sell her body. Re-visit some of your favorite characters from part 1 and see what drove them into the lifestyle that they chose. Each story different but ultimately the same.

Graphic and not for the faint of heart, the scenes take place in a realistic setting with many twist n turns you won't see coming. Find out how F.A.B Killed Sunshine and what happened in those last moments. How Green Eyes got hooked on drugs and the real reason she left Jackpot for dead in prison. Or the number one question...Will Jackpot Return To The Game?

We Keep The "P" In Publications

UPROCK
20   12
• PUBLICATIONS •

<u>Contact Joe McClain</u>

WEB: UPROCKPUBLICATIONS.COM

WEB: JOEMACUNCUT.COM

SOUNDCLOUD: SOUNDCLOUD.COM/JOE-MCCLAIN-JR

TWITTER: TWITTER.COM/JRMAC50

YOUTUBE: YOUTUBE.COM/MONEYMAC219

FACEBOOK: FACEBOOK.COM/JOEMAC619

www.ingramcontent.com/pod-product-compliance
Lightning Source LLC
Chambersburg PA
CBHW060747180626
46818CB00002B/486